LOST AND TURNED OUT

A Novel

ERNEST MORRIS

Good2Go Publishing

Author Ernest Morris
Cover design: Davida Baldwin
Typesetting: Mychea, Inc

Published 2015 by Good2Go Publishing
7311 W. Glass Lane • Laveen, AZ 85339
www.good2gopublishing.com
twitter @good2gobooks
G2G@good2gopublishing.com
Facebook.com/good2gopublishing

ThirdLane Marketing: Brian James
Brian@good2gopublishing.com

The author of the classic Flippin' Numbers series presents a new urban tale:

Lost & Turned Out

By Ernest Morris aka E.J. Morris

ACKNOWLEDGEMENTS

First and foremost, I give all glory and honors to the man above. Once again, you have blessed me with a gift to take my imagination and bring it to life. Thank you for waking me up each and every day.

I would like to once again thank all of my readers and supporters. Without you, I would have never made it to where I am today. This road has not been easy for me; but through all the adversities, I still found my way to the Promised Land.

I hope that I continue to inspire other writers to never give up on their dreams.

Thank you!

I would also like to thank everyone at the Cheesecake Factory for supporting me and my accomplishments. When I make it, we all make it.

LOST AND TURNED OUT

ONE

"HAPPY BIRTHDAY TO YOU. Happy birthday to you…" everyone sang to little Chastity at her 14th birthday party. She had been staying with her grandma ever since she was five years old After Chastity's mother died after being affected with the AIDS virus. She was strung out on drugs even before she got pregnant with Chastity.

After giving birth, it began getting even worse because her no good, baby's father ended up leaving and never came back. She found herself in all kinds of dope houses, sharing needles and having unprotected sex just to feed her addiction. Up until she died, no one knew the real reason for her sudden illness. It didn't come out until she was buried.

Chastity's grandmother, Ms. Sarah, took her in and raised her like a daughter. She would take her once a year for an HIV test to make sure that she didn't contact it during birth. Each and every time, the results came back the same: negative.

Chastity was enrolled in Bregy Elementary School to receive her education. She is now an eighth grader attending Vare Middle School on 24th Jackson Street and is doing pretty well.

"Make a wish baby and blow out the candles," her Uncle Tony said standing in back of her.

She closed her eyes, and then blew all 12 candles out as everyone clapped.

"Thank you grandma and thank you Uncle Tony for the best birthday party ever," Chastity said, giving them both a hug and kiss on the cheek.

Tony was Ms. Sarah's only remaining child. He was only 21 years old, the youngest of the three. Chastity's mom, Sabrina, was 23 when she died, and Mike had died a year ago at the age of 32. He was killed after he got into a fight at a house party. The guy waited for him outside, and when he came out, he was shot twice in the chest. He died on his way to the hospital.

Now only Tony, Ms. Sarah, and Chastity were left. Tony lived on Winter Terrace in the Wilson projects. Ms. Sarah and Chastity stayed out in west Philly on 59th and Master.

"You go and finish playing with your friends while I clean up all this cake and ice cream all over the place. Tony, you stay and help me."

"Yes, ma'am," Tony said as he began grabbing dishes off the table.

Chastity went outside with her friends to jump rope. Out of all the girls on her block, Chastity's body was far more developed than any of the others were. She stood at 4'11", already had B-cup breasts, and had a nice-shaped behind to go with it. She was so light that people swore she was white. Chastity had long hair that almost touched her butt and a face that was so beautiful that she looked like a young version of Eva Mendez.

When she walked to the store, a lot of guys that would stand on the corner would think that she was 16 or 17. Her grandma had come to the conclusion that Chastity's dad was white. Sabrina had been sleeping with so many men that it would take a lot of DNA testing to solve that puzzle.

"Come on, Chastity, it's your turn," Myia said, while turning Double Dutch.

She went over and jumped into the rope. They took turns jumping roping and playing hopscotch until it grew dark. Chastity had to go to church with her grandma in the morning, so she returned to her house.

"So did you have fun today?" Ms. Sarah asked, sitting on the couch watching television.

"Yes, I had a lot of fun, and thank you for the clothes, grandma"

"You're welcome. Sorry it's nothing all fancy and expensive, but I still have bills to pay."

The clothes Ms. Sarah brought Chastity had come from K-Mart. She was on welfare so they only gave her $320 in cash and $350 in food stamps. She made it work though, and that's all that mattered.

"Are you feeling okay, grandma? You look like you're getting sick."

"I'm fine, child! Just a little tired, so I'm going to bed now," she said, getting up and headed upstairs.

"Okay, I'll see you in the morning," Chastity said, getting ready to go take her show and go to bed.

* * *

The next morning, Chastity woke up from the sunlight beaming into her room. She looked at the clock, and saw that it was already 10:00 a.m. Usually her grandma would wake her up at 9:00 a.m. so they could catch the Sunday morning services. She jumped out of bed in her pink and white nightgown, and went to her grandma's room to wake her up.

Chastity knocked on her door, but didn't get an answer. "Grandma, are you up?" she asked, opening the door.

When she went inside, her grandma was laying there as if she was sleeping peacefully. Chastity walked over to her bed and tried to wake her up. "Grandma, it's time to get up. We're late for church."

Chastity tried shaking her but she wouldn't move. She noticed that her grandma wasn't breathing and immediately became scared. "Grandma, Grandma, wake up, please! Don't leave me grandma!" she said, shaking her and crying.

She grabbed the house phone and called 911. After she hung up the phone, she called her uncle and told him what happened. He told her that he was on his way there.

The police and fire rescue arrived 10 minutes later, and attempted CPR on her to no avail. They loaded her on the stretcher and rushed her to the hospital, all while still attempting to bring her back. Chastity rode in the ambulance with her grandma, crying the whole way to the hospital.

Ms. Sarah was pronounced DOA at 11:03 a.m. Tony arrived at the hospital five minutes afterwards, and he and Chastity stood by her bedside crying

* * *

It had been three months since the death of Chastity's grandma. They completed an autopsy on her and determined that she died in her sleep from a heart attack. Chastity took the loss hard because she had no one left but her Uncle Tony.

Tony moved her in with him at Wilson in south Philly. He didn't want to stay at his mother's house because of the memories that were left behind. Plus, it was cheaper for them to live in the projects.

It was a two-bedroom house that cost him just $190 a month. Chastity stayed in one room, and he had the other. She was closer to school now, so she didn't have to travel on the bus or wake up too early in the morning.

Her uncle spent most of his days drinking or playing cards with his friends. Chastity didn't really know anybody in the projects, so she spent most of her time in her room. When she did go outside, she would just sit on the steps and watch the other kids play.

One day, a girl named Rudy walked over to her and asked if she wanted to play with them. Two other girls came over, and she introduced them to Chastity as her sisters, Sharon and Neatra. For the next hour, they all played with Barbie dolls on the steps. The girls' mom came from the house next door to Chastity's house and told them it was time to return home.

"Bye, Chastity, we will come play with you tomorrow," Rudy said as they ran over to their mother.

Chastity went in the house, and watched her uncle and three others playing cards and drinking in the kitchen.

"Uncle Tony, can I have something to eat, please?"

"I'll make you some hot dogs and noodles after this hand is over. You can watch TV in the living room," he said.

Chastity went over to the couch and sat down to watch a couple of shows on cable. A half hour later, Tony brought food to her, and then he sat back down to continue play cards. Chastity ate her food and then went upstairs to take a shower for school the next day.

"Chastity, I'm going to be at the neighbor's house getting some drinks. I'll be back in a few, okay?"

"Yes, Uncle Tony, I'm just going to watch some more television."

Chastity watched TV for about an hour before falling asleep on the couch.

When Tony came home around 12:00 a.m., he noticed Chastity lying on the couch asleep. He was piss drunk and staggering, as he made his way over to the couch.

He sat down and looked at his niece as if she was a piece of meat. She had on her favorite pink and white nightgown. Tony could see her little white panties, so he lifted up her nightgown and stared at her for a while. He took his hand and rubbed it across her butt, while he rubbed his penis with the other. After a few minutes, Chastity woke up.

"Hey, Uncle Tony, are you okay?"

Tony moved his hand and stood up. "Come on, it's time for you to go to bed," he said, picking her up and carrying her upstairs.

5

"Do you want to sleep in the bed with your Uncle Tony tonight?" he asked her.

Chastity nodded her head yes. She didn't know any better, because she used to sleep with her grandma all the time. Tony laid her down on the bed, and stripped his clothes down to his boxers. He lay in the bed next to Chastity and put the blanket over them. Chastity closed her eyes to return to sleep when she felt her uncle hugging her from behind.

She really didn't think anything of it until he began rubbing on her chest. Her grandma never did that to her, so it was something new. When she turned on her stomach, he moved his arm.

"Don't worry little princess, I'm here with you, so go to sleep, okay?" he said, rubbing on her butt again.

Chastity laid there motionless because she didn't know what else to do. She trusted her uncle so she knew he wouldn't hurt her. She fell asleep while he continued to fondle her.

TWO

IT HAD BEEN A year and a half since little Chastity first moved in with her uncle. At 13, she had the body of a grown woman. Every night, Tony made her sleep in the room with him. He told her that it was okay for him to touch her as he did. She really believed that this was the way it was supposed to be.

One night, Tony came into Chastity's room high from smoking marijuana with his boys the entire night. She was sleeping peacefully in a pair of shorts and a t-shirt.

Tony walked up to her bed, took off his clothes, and climbed in bed with her. "Hey, my little princess! I'm here with you, okay?"

Chastity turned over on her back because she knew he wanted to play with her chest as he always did at night. It had become an every night thing, so she became used to it. She fell back asleep while he put his hands up her shirt.

A few minutes later, Chastity opened her eyes because she felt her shorts and panties being pulled off. It was dark in the room, so she couldn't see what he was doing.

She felt him opening her legs, and then his mouth was on her vagina. Chastity laid still because she didn't want to make him made. He continuously licked her between her legs, while she rubbed her chest.

After a while, Chastity felt a new feeling coming over her. She didn't know if she was about to pee on herself or if her period was coming on. "Uncle Tony, I have to use the bathroom, please," she said, trying to get up.

Tony felt her shaking, so he knew what was happening. "Just a few more minutes," he said, as he continued to lick between her thighs.

Chastity felt something that felt like chills throughout her body, and began convulsing. Tears came to her eyes as she started crying.

Tony stopped and looked up at her. "What's wrong with you, my little princess?"

"I, I, I peed on myself. I told you I had to use the bathroom, but you wouldn't let me," she said sobbing.

Tony lay next to her and gave her a hub. "You didn't pee on yourself, princess; you had your first orgasm."

"What is that?"

Tony spent the next 30 minutes answering all of little Chastity's questions about what just happened. He told her everything except the part about family is never supposed to do that to other family.

"You can never tell anybody what we do in here, okay? If you do, they will take you away from me, and I will never see you again. We are all we got. Do you understand?"

"Yes, Uncle Tony. I won't say anything," she said, as she put her panties and shorts back on before laying back down on the bed.

"That's my little princess. Tomorrow I'm going to show you the new clothes that I got for you when you start high school in a few weeks," he said, leaving the room.

Chastity lay in her bed as tears ran down her face. She knew something was wrong, because he never did what he just finished doing to her before. Her body felt unusually weird, and she never wanted to do that again.

* * *

A few weeks later, Chastity and Rudy were on their way to their first day of high school. They had been best friends ever since they met two years earlier. They both graduated from Vare with grades that allowed them to be accepted into Bok Vocational High School. Chastity was happy to be back in school, but she hated the clothes that her uncle got for her.

She had on a skirt that he got from the thrift store, a matching shirt, and a pair of Chuck Taylors. As they approached the school, Chastity noticed all the expensive-looking clothes everyone around her was wearing. Even her best friend wore designer clothes.

"I hope we have all the same classes together, so we can help each other with our homework."

"That would be cool, girl, wouldn't it?" Chastity said, as they walked passed a group of girls.

"Look at her clothes. They look like she found them in the trash," one of the girls said, causing them all to laugh.

Rudy and Chastity continued walking ignoring their cruel remarks. When they arrived at the advisory class, they realized that they had different classes. "Damn, we don't have the same classes after all. At least our lunch and gym class are together though," Rudy said.

"Well, I guess I'll see you at lunch then."

"Okay, girl, have fun and don't let those bitches get under your skin."

"I won't even pay them any attention," Chastity said, as they gave each other a hug and went into their classrooms.

Chastity was in the same class as three of the girls who made fun of her. Throughout the class, they sat behind her and called her all types of names, from nasty to trashy to dirty white girl in the hood. She felt as if she wanted to run away and cry, but she stood her ground.

When class was over, she tried rushing out the door to her next class, but she was met by the other two girls. The truth was that they were jealous of her because she was beautiful. Four of the five girls were also beautiful, but none of them had anything on Chastity. They were a few years older than she was. Chastity was too advanced for ninth-grade work, so they put her in an eleventh-grade math class in which she was doing trigonometry, figuring out with the relations between sides and angles of triangles. She began school late as a 7 year old.

"Look at the dirty white trash walking down the hall," one of the girls yelled out.

Chastity tried to ignore then, but they continued smarting off at her. She quickly grew fed up with their mouths and turned around towards them. "Fuck you, bitch! You don't even know me," she snapped at them.

They looked at her and began walking behind her. She snuck away in to the ladies room, to try to hide from them.

"That bitch has to be the dumbest girl in the school to try and hide in the bathroom," said Tanisha, one of the girls that had been harassing her, as they walked through the door.

When she saw them enter the bathroom, she tensed up out of fear.

"Talk shit now you piece of shit," Tanisha said, getting up in Chastity's face.

They surrounded her as attacking their prey would. When Tanisha took off her book bag and sat it down, she said to her friends, "Let's beat this bitch's ass, and then roll up out of her."

All the girls dropped their bags and readied to attack when the door opened. Rudy and her three sisters walked through the door. "What the fuck are y'all about to do to my little cousin," Kita, the oldest of them, said.

Tanisha, not the one to back down, stepped up. "This white piece of trash needs to watch who she's talking to!"

"From what I've heard, y'all are the one who started this shit; and just so you know, she is as black as your ugly ass. So stop calling her white," Neatra said.

10

"Y'all are not going to jump her. If you want to fight her, one on one, she will, but that's it," Kita said.

"Well, let's do it then," Tanisha said, cracking her knuckles.

Chastity had never been in a fight before, but she watched it on TV when the *Bad Girls Club* came on. She put her hands up, readying to fight.

Tanisha took the first swing. It connected with Chastity's jaw, dazing her. She shook it off as Tanisha swung again, this time missing. Chastity threw two wild punches that landed on Tanisha's mouth and eye. She then grabbed her hair and uppercut her in the face.

Chastity felt like a wild child. Kita and Rudy had to pull her off of Tanisha before she seriously hurt her. The other girls ran out of the ladies room when they saw the blood that now covered room.

Kita and the rest of her sisters also ran, as Tanisha laid on the bathroom floor, holding her face. When they made it outside, they each broke out in laughter.

"Damn, girl, you beat the shit out of her. Where did you learn how to fight like that?" Sharon asked.

Chastity's heart was still beating fast with adrenaline. After she calmed down, she said, *"Bad Girls Club."*

They all laughed again. "They wanted to jump you because you're prettier than any of those bitches," Rudy said, hugging her friend as they walked down Mifflin Street.

"We need to get you some better clothes to bring out all that beauty that you're hiding," Sharon said.

"Do you want to go to the Gallery with us?" Kita asked.

"I don't have any money."

"Neither do I? It's called five-finger discount," Rudy said with a smile.

"Don't worry, we got you this time. But the next time, you have to participate," Kita said.

11

They headed for the 47 bus stop so that they could boost some clothes from the Gallery.

* * *

"Yo, what y'all trying to do for the next couple of hours before we go meet our connect?" Hakeem asked his two friends.

"I don't know, but I don't want to sit around here, and we don't have shit to sell to these dope heads," Reese said, as they stood by Keem's Q45.

"Yeah, we can't let this shit happen again. We're losing out on a lot of money right now waiting on our connect to get back from out of town. Let's just go to the Gallery and scoop up a couple of bad bitches," Mal said.

"That sounds like a plan. Let me run in the house and grab some cash just in case I see something I like" Keem said, as he ran up in his crib on Dover Street. He grabbed a couple of stacks out of his safe and headed back out the door. "Let's roll!"

They jumped into the car and headed for the Gallery to meet some chicks.

"When are you going to trade this in for that Audi 8 that you were talking about?" Reese asked Keem.

"I'm going to look at it sometime tomorrow. You can roll with me if you want."

"That's what I'm talking about. You might be going 'dolo' though; because if we have our new product by tonight, I'll be bagging up all day tomorrow," Reese said.

"Yeah, *we* will be bagging up," Mal said correcting him.

"Fuck all this talking. Put that 2 Chains shit on and crank that shit," Keem said, as they rode down Washington Avenue.

Mal hit the play button on the iPod and they began rapping along with 2 Chains, and nodding their heads.

". . . *started from the trap, now I rap. No matter where I'm at, I got crack . . . .*"

12

* * *

Chastity was amazed as to the amount of stuff Kita and her sisters were able to steal undetected. They managed to grab all different types of skirts, jeans, and shirts. They told Chastity that they would each give her two sets apiece so that she could dress as beautiful as she looked. She was happy to have friends like them. Ever since her Uncle Tony had been doing things to her, she no longer wanted to stay in the room with him at night. She even contemplated asking her friends if their uncles did things to them at night. But she brushed off that thought because she didn't want anybody to take her away from her only living relative.

"Are you okay, Chastity?" Rudy asked, snapping her out of her thoughts.

"Yeah, I'm good. Where are we going now?" she asked as they walked.

"We're about to get something to eat from the food court. Do you want anything? I got you," Neatra asked.

"Sure, I'm starving for some pizza."

They each ordered their food and sat down to eat when they saw three handsome niggas. They walked passed them, but one of them couldn't take his eyes off of Chastity as she ate her pizza.

"Look at that nigga staring at you!" Kita said.

"Yeah, he's looking like he wants to holler at you, girl, and you don't even have your new gear on yet. Wait until everybody sees you on Monday looking fresh to death," Neatra said, bumping Chastity as they all smiled.

"Well, come on y'all, it's time to bounce so we can get back home. I still have to work later on," Kita said, as they all got up to leave.

While walking towards the exit, Keem walked over to Chastity and stood in her path so that she couldn't pass him. "Hey shorty, what's your name?"

Chastity started blushing because no boy had ever even said anything to her. "Um, Cha... Chastity."

"Well, Chastity, my name is Hakeem. Do you have a boyfriend?" he asked.

She stared at him, and out of nowhere, said "yes." She stepped to the side and caught up with her friends.

Hakeem shook his head and continued moving, while he looked for the next piece of pussy to tame.

"Girl, you're crazy! That nigga was fine. You gonna say you had a man and you don't. Have you ever even kissed a boy before?" Sharon asked.

Chastity shook her head that she hadn't and said, "I don't have time for no boys. My uncle said they just want one thing."

"You and your uncle are crazy. I would have bagged that fine-ass nigga," Sharon said.

Everybody laughed as they headed for the bus stop. Chastity thought about where she was going to tell her uncle she got all these nice clothes.

THREE

TWO MONTHS HAD PASSED since the incident in school with the girls from her class. Chastity hadn't had any problems with them since. They even attempted to speak to her when they saw her in the hallway. Everyone noticed the transformation in her appearance. Chastity appeared as if she should be on the cover of a magazine. Even her uncle noticed how attractive she had become.

He sat home watching TV when Chastity came in to the house after being outside with Rudy. She had on a pair of tights and a tight-fitting shirt that accentuated every inch of her body. She had on some Jordan's that Sharon gave to her.

"Hey, where have you been? I cooked dinner for us and there are sodas in the refrigerator."

"Thanks," she said, heading to the kitchen.

Tony watched her ass bounce back and forth with every step she took. He needed something to drink and smoke, so he went into his room and came back with a beer and a Dutch.

"Do you want some of this?" he asked Chastity, holding the Dutch in his hands.

Chastity just looked at him as if he was crazy. She hadn't allowed him in her room this past week. She told him that she was having her period so that he wouldn't touch her. It worked, but she knew she wouldn't be able to hold him off much longer.

"Uncle Tony, you now I don't do that," she lied. She had been smoking with Rudy and her sisters for a while and never tried to let her uncle catch her doing it.

"Don't lie to me, girl. I rode past you the other day and seen you out there smoking weed with your friends," Tony said, giving her a crazy stare.

She was surprised that she was caught lying, so to try to save face, she said, "I just don't feel like it right now."

"Suit yourself," he said, sitting back on the couch.

After she ate her food, she went to her room to gather her things so that she could take a shower.

Chastity jumped out of the shower and put on her nightclothes. She went into her room and sat on the bed to rub lotion on herself.

As she laid down to sleep and Tony came walking through her door. He stood there for a minute wearing nothing but boxers.

Damn, I forgot to lock my room door, she thought to herself.

Tony walked over to the bed and pulled off his boxers. She looked at him surprised, wondering what the hell he was about to do. She never had seen a man naked before, so she tensed up.

"Uncle Tony, I don't want to do that no more. Can you please get out of my room?"

"Tonight, I'm going to teach you how to become a young lady," he said while sitting down on the bed.

Chastity was scared to death because she had never seen him look at her this way before. He looked desperate and hungry for something. He moved the covers out of the way, and was about to pull her shorts off when she stopped him.

"Uncle Tony, my period is still on," she said, trying to hold her shorts from coming off.

"I'm not stupid, Chastity. It only takes up to a week for your period, unless you're on the pill or Depo, or you just had a baby."

She tried to move over to get off the bed, but he grabbed her arm and pulled her over towards him. He put his hand inside her shorts and felt her vagina. After feeling on her, he snatched her shorts and panties off.

"Please don't do this, Uncle Tony," she said through her tears.

"You're staying in my house. I'm taking care of you now, giving you food to eat, and clothes to put on your back. This is the least you can do to show me your appreciation. Either you do what I want, or you can pack your shit and get the fuck out. Matter of fact, I gave all that shit to you, so leave it here," he said, staring at her.

Chastity couldn't believe the nerve of him. He was treating her as if she wasn't even his family. She didn't want to get kicked out because there would be no place to go. At the same time, she wasn't going to allow her uncle rob her of her virginity.

"I thought you loved me, Uncle Tony. But because I'm not willing to give myself to you, you're kicking me out? I'll leave, and you will never have to worry about me again," she said, putting on her clothes to leave.

As she walked down the steps towards the door, Tony came after her and stopped her. "If you tell anybody what went on in this house, I will hurt you. Do you understand me?"

She nodded her head, as tears fell from her eyes. She knew at that moment that he really didn't love her. He was just using her.

"When you realize that it's a cold world out there, and nothing is given to you for free, then you can come back and I might let you back in," he said, opening the door for her.

Chastity walked out and realized it was raining. "Can I have my umbrella, please Uncle Tony?"

The door slamming in her face was the only response she received. She began walking down the block towards the end of the Terrace. The rain was only coming down in a drizzle, but it was enough to soak her clothes.

As Chastity walked, a car sped past her and then suddenly stopped. The driver backed up and rolled down the window.

"Hey beautiful, I thought that was you. Why are you out here at 10:00 at night, walking in the rain?" he asked.

Chastity looked up and saw that it was the good-looking guy from the Gallery that tried talking to her.

"Please go away. I don't want to talk to anybody right now."

Keem sensed something was wrong and stepped out of the car with his umbrella. He walked over to Chastity and put it over her head. Keem didn't like to comfort chicks. All he wanted to do was fuck 'em and keep it moving. Chastity was something special, and he wanted to get to know her.

"Where is your boyfriend now so I can fuck him up for making you walk in the rain?"

She looked at him puzzled for a moment, and then realized that she told him that at the Gallery.

"I don't have a boyfriend. I was lying," she admitted.

"So who in the world would have you out here like this in the rain by yourself? Do you need a ride home? I know your parents must be sick and worried about you right now."

"My parents are dead, and my Uncle Tony kicked me out because I ..." Her tears cut off her from finishing the sentence.

Keem couldn't believe that someone so beautiful was all alone like this. Feeling sorry for her, he decided to comfort her.

"Get in the car. You're going to come stay with me for as long as you like. Fuck your uncle! The nigga probably never cared about you anyway," he said, opening the passenger door for Chastity.

At first, she was scared to go with this stranger, fearing that he might try to kill her. She knew that it was chilly outside and she had nowhere else to go. Reluctantly, she got inside the car and closed the door.

Keem made his way back into the driver's seat and passed her a jacket from the backseat. He turned the heat up to war her up.

"How old are you, shorty?" he asked.

"15."

He looked at her surprised like hell. "No seriously, what's your age for real?"

"I said I'm 15 years old. What, you don't believe me or something?" she asked, becoming more comfortable in the seat.

"I just can't believe that someone with a body like yours is only 15. I thought you were like 18 or 19."

"How old are you?" Chastity wanted to know.

"I'm only 20. I'll be 21 next week, though. I have my own crib on Dover Street. It's a two-bedroom, small row house. So you will be able to have all the privacy you need."

"Why are you doing this for me?"

"Because I know what it feels like to be out on the streets with no one to turn to. Plus, you're so beautiful. I wouldn't dare let somebody else scoop you up. Now just sit back and relax. I got you, baby girl."

*   *   *

When they arrived at Hakeem's house, he parked and quickly made his way out of the car. "Come on in, it's safe," Keem said smiling.

Chastity hesitated for a moment because this was all new to her, so she was scared to follow him in. She hesitantly stepped out of the car and followed him inside.

Inside the house appeared surprisingly nice for a 20-year-old's place. It had a beautiful living room set, and the kitchen was basic. He showed her the two room upstairs, the bathroom, and the backyard.

"That room next to the bathroom is yours. It's small, but you will like it. That is a full size bed, so you have plenty of room to roll around," he said smiling.

Keem looked at her body and couldn't help but think how it would feel to be fucking her right then. Her age was what was stopping him. He wasn't trying to go to jail for molesting a minor.

"Thank you, but I don't have anything to wear, and these clothes are still wet."

"Take your shower and go in my room. Look in the closet, and find a pair of my ball shorts to wear. There are t-shirts in my dresser. You can hang your wet clothes up in your room. Tomorrow, I will take you clothes shopping so that you will have something to wear for school on Monday. What school do you go to?"

"Bok Vocational. I'm in the 9th grade. My friend, Rudy, goes there, too, and we always ride together," she said.

"Okay, we'll pick her up, and I'll drop both of you off. Now, go get out of those wet clothes while I go take care of something in the basement. If you need anything, just knock on the door," he said, heading back downstairs.

Chastity went in Keem's room to find something to wear, and she noticed how many clothes he had in his closet. They were everywhere, and shoeboxes were stacked up along the wall. Altogether, she counted 52 pairs of shoes and sneakers together. The bed was so big that it could hold six people compared to hers at home that barely held her, let along her uncle when he snuck in there at night.

She grabbed the clothes and left the room. After she took her shower and put the dry clothes on, she lay on the bed and drifted off to sleep.

Keem was in the basement counting money and readying the packages of dope for him and his boy. He was talking to Mal on the phone about what they were going to do the next day.

"We have to step up our game. I mean, we're only making a few dollars while our connect is getting paid," Mal said.

"So what do you want to do then? It's not as if we're balling and shit. That couple of stacks that we make a week ain't shit compared to what we could be making!"

"Exactly, so let's ask for more product."

"I'll talk to Chris tomorrow about it. But we are going to be on the block tomorrow going hard 'cause I'm about to spend a stack on shopping in the morning," Keem said, putting the money back in the safe.

"What are you buying now, nigga? You have enough shit in you damn closet to last you a lifetime," Mal said laughing.

"It's not for me, nigga. It's for this lil' shorty I met when we were at the Gallery the other day. She's going to be staying with me for a while. She don't have anywhere to go because her uncle kicked her out," Keem said.

"That's fucked up! What was she doing... tricking or something? You know she had to be doing something out there."

"I haven't gotten the full story yet, but I will. I'll tell you about it tomorrow. I'm about to get some rest, so we can grind hard tomorrow."

"Yeah, yeah nigga. I bet you'll be resting. Resting in some of that yellow pussy," Mal smirked.

"Fuck you, nigga. See you later," Keem said while hanging up the phone.

FOUR

"OH, SHIT, BABY, YOUR dick is so big. Tear this pussy up! It's all yours. Yes, baby! I'm about to cum," Kita screamed as some nigga was fucking the shit out of her.

He was fucking her doggy style while Rudy watched from the closet. They didn't even know she was in the room. She wanted to see if her sister had grabbed the Prada belt that she snatched from the mall. Before she could leave, Kita and her friend walked in, and began going at it. Rudy still hid in the closet and watched as he lifted up her skirt and began fucking her.

Rudy's pussy was dripping wet as he watched the boy's dick go in and out of her sister. She tried to close her legs to keep her juices from running down them. She only had a towel on because she had just gotten out of the shower.

"Ummmmm, damn girl, your pussy is so good. Lay your ass on the bed," he said, as he pulled his pants all the way off.

Kita pulled her panties off and lay on the bed, spreading her legs open. The dude got down on his knees and started eating Kita's pussy. He had her legs on his shoulders, going to work.

"Ahhhhh, shit! Eat this pussy, nigga. God damnnnn, I shouldn't have been letting you eat this good shit," Kita said while on the verge of another orgasm.

Rudy's eyes grew big, as she watched this live porno session going on in her sister's room.

"Yesssss, oh baby! Let me feel that dick in this pussy again, so I can cum all over your shit!"

He stood up, pulled her legs back to her head, and then stuck his dick inside her pussy.

"That's it! Fuck me harder... faster... harder... faster. Yes, right there! Oh, I'm cummming!" Kita screamed, as she shot her load all over his dick.

Rudy watched the action without noticing that the closet door opened slightly. Her towel was now on the floor.

The dude was still trying to get his shit off, when he noticed Rudy in the closet watching. A smile came on his face when he saw that she was naked.

Rudy saw him staring at her and became nervous that he would give her up. She just continued to watch as his dick went in and out of her sister's pussy.

He whispered something to her, and began making circular motions with his tongue. As he was showing it to Rudy, he began fucking Kita faster until he pulled out of her and busted his load all over her stomach.

"Damn, that shit was good. I'm ready for another round of that good shit, are you?" he said to Kita.

"I can't, I'm already late for work. Maybe we can meet up when I get off work. I'm gonna go take a quick shower. You can let yourself out," Kita said, as she threw on a robe and left the room to take a shower.

As soon as she shut the door, the dude walked over to the closet and opened the door. "Damn, your body is nice," he said, standing there looking at Rudy's naked body. "Did you enjoy the show?"

Rudy grabbed her towel off the floor, wrapping it around her body, as she stepped out of the closet.

She stared at his still erect dick and licked her lips, without noticing that he was still staring at her. As she made her way to the door, he grabbed his clothes and began putting them on.

"I want some of that," he said.

Rudy smiled and walked out the door. She went to her room and jumped on the bed. She began fingering her pussy, wishing it were that dude's mouth.

The dude left Kita's room and walked down the hall when he heard a moaning noise. He stopped and cracked open the door, watching Rudy play with herself while her eyes were closed.

Thinking he had another chance, he looked around, making sure that Kita was still in the bathroom. He then snuck in the room, closed the door, and locked it.

Rudy opened her eyes and jumped up covering herself. "What are you doing in my room?"

"I know you were thinking about this just now, so let me taste that," he said, pulling out his dick.

She looked at him without saying anything while he walked over and pulled the sheet off of her. He pushed her back onto the bed and knelt down onto his knees. He opened her legs and started eating her pussy.

Rudy closed her eyes and grabbed his head, enjoying the sensation that was taking over her body. This was her first time allowing someone to eat her pussy. She heard about it and had seen it on TV, but never had the chance to experience the real thing until now. She even had sex with her boyfriend before, but not this.

"You like that shit, don't you?" he asked her.

She couldn't say anything but "yes," as he continued to make magic to her love box.

"I'm about to cum, please don't stop. Oh my, I'm cummmming," Rudy screamed and she tried to run, but he gripped her waist as she came all in his mouth.

"Damn, girl, you tasted so good. Can I get a sample of that pussy now?"

"No, but maybe some other time. You have to go before my sister catches you in here. What is your name, anyway?" she asked, putting on her shirt and shorts.

"Reese," he smiled, putting his dick back in his pants. He gave her his number. "Call me if you want to get together again. Your sister is just someone I pay for sex, but I want to do more for you. Only if you with it," he said, leaving the room.

Rudy sat on the bed and smiled. "Whewwww," was all she could say after experiencing the head job she just received.

* * *

Keem left the house early because his connect wanted to meet up with him. He already knew what the meeting was going to be about. He just didn't expect it to come so early in the morning. He left a stack on the table for Chastity to shop for clothes with.

He never gave a chick more than $50 unless he was fucking her, and here he was giving up a thousand dollars to a girl that he only met twice. The worst part was she was only 15 years old. She turned 16 in a month, from what she told him during the conversation he had with her that morning.

Keem couldn't stop thinking about how beautiful she was, so he decided that he would use her to his advantage. First, he had to determine if she was willing to be his mule or not. He would discuss that tonight when he returned home.

He called Mal to see where he was. "You picked a fine time to call back now, nigga!" Mal said.

"Man, shut up! Where you at right now?"

"I'm at the spot taking care of that work. Why, what's up?"

"I was trying to call you last night so we could kick it with some broads I had from the projects. When you didn't answer, I called Reese and we rolled out."

25

"I was chilling at the crib. But listen... my connect just called me, and he wants to meet up with me this morning. You know what this is going to be about, so I will let you know what happens," Keem said.

"Okay, I hope everything goes right. If you need me, just hit me up on the jack. I'm about to hit the block to get this money."

"Okay, let me call Reese and fill him in," Keem said, hanging up.

Keem dialed Reese's number, and he picked up on the third ring. "Yizzo, what's up, cannon?"

"What good my nigga, where you at?"

"I just left this chick's crib. Listen to this shit though. I'm fucking the bitch in her room, and the whole time her sister was in the closet watching us. She as bad as shit too. After I fucked her sister, I went in the other room and tried to pop her too. She wouldn't let me though. She only let me eat that shit. I can tell she hasn't had any real dick yet; but don't worry, I'm a tear that ass up when I get the chance," Reese excitedly said.

"You one wild nigga, but anyway, I'm meeting with the connect in a few minutes. Mal is at the crib, so go over there and help him out. I will come through when I'm done," Keem said.

"Alright, see you later."

Once Keem ended his call with Reese, he left to meet up with his connect. He was going to call Chastity and see if she was okay, but she didn't have a phone. He decided to pick one up for her on his way back.

* * *

Hakeem and his connect met at 31st and Grays Ferry in the Pathmark parking lot. He saw him pull up in an all-white Maserati with dark tint. Hakeem exited out of his car and jumped into the Maserati.

"What's up with you, lil nigga?" Chris asked as they shook hands.

"I'm chilling. Trying to get this money so that I can cop one of these things like you."

"In time, my nigga, in time. Anyway, I was talking to my brother, and he wants to hit you off with some shit that will keep you fully stocked so you can make a lot money. Can you handle that type of work?"

Keem was surprised because he thought they were going to cut him off because they found out he was looking for a new supplier. Now they were offering him more product.

"I can handle it, if that's what y'all want to do. You supply me with the best heroin in the country, but I thought it was limited. That's why I was looking for another connect," Keem said.

"I'm not mad at you for that but next time come to me and let me know that you need more. We supply most of the East Coast, so why wouldn't I have enough for your small-time ass!"

Hakeem felt slightly disrespected but he brushed it off. He knew Chris was right because they were only copping 1,000 bundles at a time.

"So how much more are you willing to give us?" he asked.

"We are going to give you 1,500 bundles, and if you can off that within four days, we will up it to 2,000 bundles. I want to see if you can move some coke as well, but you will have to pay for that up front. I'll let you know when I get a price for you. So are you good with that?" Chris asked.

"Yeah, that's music to my ears. I'll let my boys know that we are moving up a little. When can we get the product?"

"After you knock off what you have, I will hit you with the new work. Make sure that you come with every dime,

27

because we're not taking short money any more. Call me when you're ready."

Chris shook Keem's hand as he got out of the car. Keem was excited about the new deal. He couldn't wait to let his boys know what was happening.

Before Chris pulled off, he rolled down his window and shouted, "Hakeem." When he turned around, Chris continued, "If we hear that you're looking for a new connect again you will be cut off and you won't be selling anything on these streets again."

He rolled the window back up as he drove down and out of the parking lot, leaving the threat to simmer through Keem's head.

FIVE

CHASTITY SAT IN THE living room on the ottoman talking to Rudy after returning from shopping at the mall.

"Damn girl, you have a lot of clothes to wear now and you only had to spend four hundred dollars," Rudy said.

"I know. Thanks to all the stuff that you and your sisters taught me, I can get anything I want. I can't believe that he gave me a thousand dollars just like that to shop with."

"You must have sucked the shit out of his dick last night for him to basically move you in his little crib."

"No, that shit is nasty, girl!" Chastity said as she frowned her face.

Well then, you must have fucked the shit outta him," Rudy said laughing.

"Damn, you are so loquacious today. For your information, I'm not fucking or sucking anybody. I've never even done that before. So there you have it! Have you ever done it before?"

"What have you been doing, studying the dictionary trying to use big words instead of getting your lil' coochie touched? You mean to tell me that no one popped your cherry yet?" Rudy asked.

Chastity's laugher made Rudy laugh as well. "I never got to do any of that shit yet. I've only seen a penis once. That shit was big as hell, too. How do they put all of that inside of you without it hurting?"

"You are too smart to be so dumb. I can tell you this though, that shit feels so good. My sister Sharon taught me everything I know. She used to let me watch her and her boyfriend have sex. I would hide in the closet so that he couldn't see me. She taught me how to suck a dick and how to ride one. I was in Kita's room this morning and couldn't get out while she and this dude were getting it on. Girl, I was scared that they were going to catch me, but they didn't," Rudy said, leaving out the part that he had seen her.

"Can you teach me how to suck a dick?"

"Come on, let's go to my house and my sister can teach you. They are the experts in that, plus they can give you the scoop on niggas. Put you up on game, you feel me?" Rudy said, putting her coat on.

"Let me leave a message for Keem, so he knows that I'm gone," Chastity said, writing something down on paper.

"Girl, you don't have to let niggas know anything. If he want to be able to contact you, let him buy you a cell phone. Let's go!"

Chastity and Rudy left the house making their way for the bus stop.

* * *

When they got to Rudy's house, everybody was gone except Neatra who was cooking. They had been on their own since they were kicked out by their mom. Since Kita was the oldest at 20, she was able to get a house through Philadelphia Housing Authority (PHA). The rent was only $97 a month, which she paid without problem.

Sharon and Kita worked at Bayada Nurses, and Neatra and Rudy collected social security checks every month for their deceased father. The streets practically raised them.

"... *Dripping down his dick, this pussy too vicious. Every time I fuck him, I say, 'Who's is it?'*" Nicki Minaj was blaring throughout the stereo system, as Neatra took the fried chicken out of the pot.

"What you bitches doing here?" she said smiling.

"Chas needs our help, so I brought her here. Since Kita and Sharon aren't here, we have to show her."

30

"What are we showing her now?" Neatra said, turning the burner off on the stove.

Rudy smiled, "How to perform a perfect blow job that would make a nigga's toes curl up!"

"So who you trying to impress, Chas?"

Chastity sat at the table and said, "Nobody, I just want to learn some shit for future reference. I never done that before."

"Shit, the bitch never had sex before," Rudy said.

"Get the fuck out of here! You mean to tell me that we have a virgin in our presence? So what do you want to know, because Kita and Sharon are the pros? They taught us everything we know."

"I just want to get some insight on giving a blow job," Chastity said.

"We can teach you the art of seduction. We have it all on the internet," Neatra said.

"Let's see it then."

They made their way over to the computer to watch a few videos on oral sex.

"You mean to tell me that none of the boys in your school haven't even ate your kitty either?"

Chastity thought about what her uncle used to do to her at night while watching the guy on the screen go to work on the girl's pussy. She realized that she had been having oral sex for a while now. It just really disappointed her that it was with her uncle.

"No, that's why I'm here," she said laughing.

The girls watched a few videos of Superhead and some other shit for an hour. Kita and Sharon arrived home and they began talking about Chastity being a virgin among other things. Kita said she would show her the basics tomorrow because she was tired. She left them sitting in the kitchen.

Then Sharon had an idea. "I got you, girl!" she said, as she took a banana from the fruit bowl on the table. "Take this and pretend it's a penis. Now I want you to do everything you saw that girl doing."

Chastity took the banana and began licking the tip, and then she put it in her mouth, and moved it in and out like it was a real dick. It was fun for a while, but she wanted to do it for real.

"Okay, I got it now, but I need to try it for real now. Plus, I'm also trying to do the sex thing," Chastity said, as they sat at the kitchen table.

"Don't rush into have sex. That will be your worst mistake, especially if it's just any random person. Make sure it's with somebody that you like," Sharon said getting up from the table. "Now if y'all will excuse me, my man is outside. I'm about to get my back dug out. See you later."

Sharon left through the backdoor and jumped into the car with her boyfriend.

After Chastity used Rudy's phone, they sat on the couch to talk for a while.

"I have about two hours before Keem picks me up, so what do you want to do?"

"Let's go up to Sharon's room and I'll show you the dildos she be using with her freaky ass," Rudy excitedly said.

"Now, I don't want to mess with that shit. Let's watch some more videos," Chastity said.

They watched the videos until Keem arrived to take her home. She road home with one thing on her mind.

* * *

When they got home, Keem went to his room to change his clothes. Chastity sat on the couch watching *Bad Girls Club*. She saw her bag on the chair containing the shorts that she bought at the mall.

She grabbed a pair from the bag and laid them on the couch to wear to bed. She looked around to see if Keem was coming back down yet, and when she didn't see him, she started to change hr clothes.

Chastity took off her jeans and saw that her panties were wet. She knew it was from watching the pornos. In a way, she wanted to do those things she had seen. She wished that it were Keem instead of her uncle that introduced her to that. She started taking off her panties to put on the shorts, when Keem came downstairs.

He looked at her ass and his dick grew rock hard. It poked out of his shorts so far that when Chastity turned around, he couldn't hide it. Her pussy was phat and hairy because she didn't shave.

"Umm, excuse me! Finish getting dressed," he said, as he ran back up the stairs.

Chastity put her shorts on and then went up to her room. Keem met her as he exited the bathroom.

"I got you this phone so you don't have to use somebody else's," he said, passing her the new Galaxy S5.

"Oh, my God! Thank you, Keem," she said, giving him a hug.

"No problem! I'm going to get something to drink. Do you want anything?"

"No, I'm just going to put my stuff away," Chastity said, going into her room.

After putting her clothes away, she began programming numbers in her phone. She even put her Uncle Tony's number in there. Even though she hated him for what he did, he was still her only remaining family.

She called Rudy, but didn't get an answer, so she texted her, Sharon, Neatra, and Kita with her new number.

It was 11:30 p.m. so she decided to lay down and get some sleep for school the next morning. As soon as her head hit the pillow, she was out.

* * *

"I knew I would find your ass. What you thought, that you could hide from me? Now I'm going to take what I want and there's nothing that you can do about it," Tony said, laying in the bed behind Chastity.

She tried to scream, but nothing came out because his hand covered her mouth.

He removed her shorts and entered her from behind. He began pumping faster and harder with each thrust. His grip was so tight that she couldn't break free.

"That's right, take this dick, girl! I always knew this pussy could be this good. Oh shit baby, you are so wet. Let me stick this dick in that fat ass of yours," Tony said, as he pulled out of her and keeping his hand over her mouth.

Chastity was in so much pain that she just wanted it all to be over with.

"If you're gonna keep quiet I'll let you go."

Chastity shook her head in agreement, trying not to give in to her uncle taking advantage of her.

As soon as he let go of her mouth, she screamed at the top of her lungs. "Please help me, Hakeem, help!"

Tony just laughed at her and pointed at the door, where Keem's dead body lied. "It's just me and you, and I'm going to fuck you all night long, so stop fighting it," he said, laughing as he entered Chastity again from behind.

"Chastity, Chastity, Chastity! Wake up ma; you're having a bad dream!" Keem said while shaking her.

She quickly sat up screaming and sweating. It took her a couple of minutes to realize she was dreaming.

"Are you okay? Who was trying to hurt you? You can tell me," he said, as he put his arm around her.

Chastity cried for a few minutes because she really thought her uncle came to hurt her.

"You're safe here, ma. I will never let anybody hurt you again, okay?"

Chastity put her head in his chest and felt safe. "I want to sleep in the room with you tonight."

"Sure, come on," Keem said, as they went to his room.

They laid in the bed and Chastity began rubbing his dick, bringing it to life.

"Whoa, ma! What are you doing? You're too young for this right now," Keem said as he sat up.

"I'm not a child anymore. Those days were over when I stepped out on my own. If you don't want to be my first then I'll find someone who will," she said, staring at him with eyes that could kill.

"Wait, you're a virgin? Don't you want your first time to be special and with the person you love?" he asked.

"Fuck all that bullshit! Love don't live here anymore. Now, are you going to pop this cherry or am I going to get it done elsewhere?'

That dream triggered something inside of her and it caused her to become one cold-hearted bitch. Kita had been teaching her how to manipulate niggas to get what she wanted. She told her the power of the pussy is genuine. She stood off from the bed and removed her shorts. She then took off her shirt and lay back on the bed.

"I'm trying to show my loyalty to you. You've been so nice to me and you gave me more than anybody ever gave me. I just want to know what it feels like to have sex," Chastity said while lying there.

"Let me make love to you then. It will be so much better."

She sat up and said, "What is making love? I was told that people have sex and get paid, then leave out of there richer than you came in with." "Who in the hell is feeding you all these lies? I'm not gonna take your virginity like this. That would make me feel like I'm taking advantage of you," he said while covering her up.

35

Keem got up out of the bed and looked at her. "I'm going to sleep in your room tonight. You stay in here and maybe we can try against tomorrow."

He walked out the door smiling because with a little more time, he knew that he would be molding her into the soldier that he needed. He just had to keep showing her what a good life is. He still needed to figure out where he was going to get the money needed to buy more product.

SIX

A MONTH LATER, EVERYTHING was cool with Chastity and Keem. They slept in the same bed, but he never tried anything. He was trying to groom her into the person he wanted her to be. Little did he know that she was also getting schooled by her friends.

For her birthday, he took her on a shopping spree to Atlantic City. No one had ever done the things that he was doing for her before. Keem had even put his car on hold so that he could shower her with gifts. Instead of fucking her body, he was fucking her mind, and she was too naïve to realize it.

The things that Kita and Sharon were showing her were all about using what you got to get what you want. Hakeem was showing her the fast life and the ease of blowing money. He needed her to be willing to do anything to be able to continue blowing money at will.

He thought the time was right to put the icing on the cake. He thought that once he had sex with her, he could get her to do anything that he wanted her to do. Her mind was his for the picking. Since she was only 16, he had to be careful who knew what was going on between them.

As they lied in bed watching TV, Keem moved over closer to Chastity and put his arm around her.

"Baby girl, are you ready to give me that sweet pussy of yours? I'm tired of waiting and so is he," Keem said pointing to his erection.

Chastity was fully prepared for this, thanks to her friends who had let her watch them fuck random niggas and show her how to seduce men in bed. Truth be told, she was about to fuck some nigga that Rudy had introduced her to. He lived in the projects and sold drugs on the block. She was just tired of waiting for Keem to do it. She wanted to see what it felt like to have sex.

"I've been ready," she said, as she started removing her clothes.

"No, chill out! I got this," Keem said, as he started kissing her. He got on top of her and began kissing her neck, working his way down her body.

He came back up and started kissing her again, but this time he slipped his tongue into her mouth. Chastity didn't know what to do so she just followed his lead.

Keem started taking off his clothes one at a time and threw them on the floor. Next, he pulled Chastity's shirt over her head displaying her perky nipples. Then he pulled off her shorts and panties all at the same time.

She lay back down as he began licking her body from top to bottom, starting with her titties. They were nice, full-size breasts. She had the body of a grown woman and he was going to treat her that way.

He cupped one of her breasts and put it in his mouth, sucking on her for a few minutes before switching.

Chastity had never felt this way before. She felt herself becoming wet below. All the schooling provided to the girls wasn't enough to come close to what she was feeling.

He continued licking her body until he reached her inner thighs. Keem was so overwhelmed by the heat coming from her pussy that he now had to have her. There was no turning back. He began massaging her clit with his tongue.

"Mmmmm, oh God, that feels good!" Chastity said, remembering how Kita and Sharon said it would feel. She began experiencing the feeling that she had only one time previously, but this time she knew what was about to happen.

"I'm cumming, Keem. Oh shit!" she said, as he continued licking and playing with her nipples.

Keem slid his body up and started kissing her, letting her taste her juices. "Are you ready for this?" he said, rubbing the tip of his dick on her pelvis.

"Yes, baby, I'm ready," she said opening her legs wider.

Keem began to push the head in slow and easy. She grabbed him around the neck as more and more of him eased in.

"Owwww," she said, as tears came to her eyes.

"Do you want me to stop?"

"No, keep going. I want all of you inside me," she said, wrapping her legs around his body.

Keem slowly began to pump in and out of her, and slowly began speeding up the thrusts. To his surprise, Chastity started pumping back meeting his every thrust. The pain became pleasure to her and she was beginning to enjoy it with him.

"I'm about to bust, baby girl," Keem said, pumping harder and faster until he couldn't hold it any longer.

He pulled out and bust all over her stomach. She remembered what Kita said to do afterwards, so she took her hand and rubbed it all over her body. Then she licked her fingers.

"Ummm," she said, sucking on her finger. "You taste and feel so good. Now lay down and let me get on top," she said.

Keem and Chastity spent the next four hours fucking as if they were wild animals. He tried to teach her everything he knew and she was trying to show him that she was a quick learner.

* * *

The next morning Hakeem and Chastity were cuddled up in bed when he received a call from Chris. "Hello," he groggily said.

"You up, nigga? Come outside. I need to holla at you for a minute!"

"Alright, here I come now," Keem said, getting out of bed.

As soon as he jumped in the car, Chris pulled off and parked on the next block.

"I want you to take a trip for me to Miami this weekend. You will need to take someone with you who you trust to carry the work back on their body. I prefer it be a girl, because they are less likely to get searched. You will be meeting my supplier out there and he will give you six keys to bring back," he said, making sure Keem was paying attention.

"Once you get to the airport, someone will be there to take you to the hotel that I booked for you. My supplier will contact you when he's ready to see you. I'm going to give you half of a key in return on consignment. Do you want this or not?"

"What happened to your other runners?" Keem said, curious to know.

"One of them got pinched a week ago coming home from the airport, so I have to replace him. I would like to use you temporarily for the next few runs until I find a suitable replacement," Chris said, looking at Keem.

"How long will I be gone?"

"Two days tops. Once you and your mule get there, you will have fun and enjoy yourselves for a day; then the next day you'll handle your business and return home. It's just that simple."

Keem thought about it for a moment. He figured that if he took Chastity, he could fuck her the whole time and make her believe that he took her on a vacation. Then he could manipulate her into carrying the work back for him.

"I'll do it," he said, thinking about the come-up that he would make off of it.

"Good" Chris simply said, as he drove around the block and dropped off Keem in front of his door.

Keem went back in the house and ran upstairs to this room. Chastity was putting on a pair of boy shorts when he walked into the room.

"You're not dressed yet? Keep playing around and you're gonna be late for school."

"You're the one that's going to make me late by keeping me up all night. Besides, I'll be ready in 15 minutes. I just have to fix my hair and brush my teeth," Chastity said, heading towards the bathroom.

"Wait, I have to ask you something. How would you like to take a trip to Miami with me this weekend?"

Chastity looked at him with excitement lining her face. "For real? I would love to go there. How long will we be going?"

"Only two days because you have to be back by Monday for school," Hakeem said, putting on some clothes to drop off Chastity and Rudy at school.

"Okay, I have to tell Rudy that we can't go to the mall this weekend. She will probably still go without me anyway, but oh well, I'm going to Miami," Chastity said, dancing around the room.

This was the first time she had ever left Philly. No one ever showed her this much luxury before in her life. She now had designer clothes, name-brand shoes, money in her pocket, and the list seemed to never end. One thing was for certain, she was beginning to get turned on by all the gifts and being treated so nice. She never wanted to go back to that broke, thrift store clothes-wearing person that she used to be.

Fifteen minutes later, they were in Keem's car heading to Wilson to grab Rudy and Neatra for school. After he dropped them off, Keem was going to head over to the spot where he would let his boys know about the upcoming weekend.

* * *

"Hakeem wants me to go to Miami with him on Friday so that we can enjoy the sun. What do you think about that?"

"Girl, I think you must have been putting it on him last night that he wants to take you to Miami. That's my fucking dog," Neatra said, as they all laughed while they stood in front of Rudy's locker.

"Damn, I wish I could sit on a beach all day and enjoy the sun like you're gonna be doing," Rudy said.

"How about I ask him if you can come with us? After all, you are my best friend," Chastity said.

"No, girl, that is y'all chance to be alone and get your freak on. Just take lots of pictures and send them to my phone, especially of those sexy ass niggas that will be walking around shirtless."

"I got you! Let me get to class before I'm late. I'll see you at lunch time," Chastity said.

I won't be there. I have a date with this sexy nigga. I'm leaving now because he's outside waiting for me," Rudy said, with a smile on her face.

"You are one nasty bitch. Go ahead and handle yours and I'll see you when I get home," Chastity said, rushing to class.

Rudy walked outside looking around for her date. When she spotted Reese standing next to his Dodge Charger, she smiled and walked over towards him.

"I didn't think you were going to call me with your sex ass. I was starting to miss that sweet taste," Reese said.

Rudy smirked, "Well, show me how much you missed it. Where are we going to go? My sister is at my crib."

"We can go chill at my house on 20th and Mountain. Hop in so I can touch on something."

"As long as that paper is right, you can touch it all," she said, shutting the car door.

"That's definitely not a problem!"

* * *

When they stepped inside Reese's crib, Mal was sitting on the couch playing X-box. Reese greeted him and winked his eye.

"Do you want something to drink?"

"A soda is cool with me if you have any," Rudy said, sitting on the couch where Mal was.

Reese went into the kitchen and grabbed a grape soda out of the refrigerator. He looked in the cabinet, pulled out a skinny pill bottle, and went back to the living room

He passed her the soda and sat down next to her. "Have you ever popped any molly?"

"No, but I tried 'E' pills before."

"It's the same thing as 'E.' Do you want one?" Reese said, passing her one.

She took it, trying to show him that she was a big girl and not one of those scared-ass young girls. After she swallowed it, she drank the soda to wash it down. She then sat back and watched the two boys play a game of *Call of Duty*.

After they finished the first game, Reese could see that the molly had started kicking in. He started rubbing on her breast and kissing her neck.

"How about you let me and my man hit that?" he asked, still rubbing on her breast.

"As long as that check is right, I'm down for whatever. Pay like you weigh, nigga," she said, holding her hand out.

Rudy already knew what it was hitting when she walked in and saw Mal sitting there. That's why, when Reese offered her a molly; she said it."

They both peeled off a hundred dollars and gave it to her, "Fuck her. She stood up and unbuttoned her jeans, pulling them off.

Reese loved the sight of her neatly shaved pussy, staring at it as she took off her panties.

Mal pulled his dick out, as she kneeled down and took him in her mouth. She began sucking his dick as if she was a professional.

Reese got behind her and started eating her pussy from the back. Her shit felt so wet he thought as he licked all over her clit. He took two fingers and started fucking her pussy while he sucked up all juices.

Mal was enjoying the way she was sucking his dick. Her mouth felt like a warm pussy. He grabbed her head and started fucking her mouth until he felt himself about to bust.

She felt it, too, so she pulled out his dick and let his nut shoot all over her face.

Reese stood up, put on a condom, and then entered her from behind. He started off slow and then began speeding up, hitting her walls with every thrust.

"Oh, shit, yes! Give it to me," she screamed, as she took Mal's dick back into her mouth.

She was really into it now, thanks to the mollies. She was so turned on now that she started throwing it back as Reese pounded out her pussy.

Reese was ready to cum, so he pulled out, and took the condom off.

Mal put one on and told her to sit on his dick. Rudy sat down backwards as Mal lifted her up and down on his dick.

She grabbed Reese's dick and started sucking it until he shot his load all down her throat. They took turns fucking Rudy in multiple positions for hours, until it was time to take her home.

When the molly wore off, she felt entirely drained out. Her pussy was so sore that she thought she wouldn't have sex for a week. She didn't care as long as she recieved her money.

Kita and Sharon had molded her into a true get-money bitch. She wanted to be just like them, so it wasn't difficult to not follow in their footsteps. They had everything they wanted, and one nigga was about to pay for Kita's car.

They dropped Rudy off at home and she went in the house, took a quick shower, and then lay down until she heard from her friend. She promised herself that she wasn't going to take Reese seriously now. If he wanted her to be his girl, then he wouldn't have let his man hit it. All he wanted was some pussy and he could get it every time as long as the money was coming in.

SEVEN

CHASTITY AND HAKEEM WERE walking out of the airport lobby when they noticed a man standing next to a Lincoln town car. He was holding up a sign with Hakeem's name on it. They walked over to him, passed their bags to him, and then got into the car. He put the bags in the trunk, and then jumped in the driver's seat to take them to the hotel.

As they rode down Sunset Boulevard, Chastity looked out of the window in amazement at all the fancy cars and people that were out.

"Look at that Aston Martin, right there. I know whoever is driving that shit is paid," Keem said.

As they passed it by, a female stepped out of the driver's seat and another one-stepped out of the passenger's side.

"That has to be her man's shit right there. There's no way she's getting that kind of money."

"Actually that belongs to her, and she has two others just like it, but different colors," the driver said.

Chastity was impressed by the lady who looked no more than 30. She wanted to live that lifestyle one day.

The driver pulled into the Marriott Hotel and began taking their bags out of the trunk. "Here is your room key, sir. You have a suite on the 11th floor, complements of Mr. Pedro. He would like for you to meet him at the club tonight so that y'all can talk."

"Which club and what time?"

"Club Bamboo. You can get there between 11:00 and 1:00, if you want to catch him before he started conducting business. A car will pick you up when you're ready, unless you choose to drive yourself."

I'll take a driver because I wouldn't know where I'm going anyway. Tell him to pick us up from the lobby at 10:30," Keem said, as they headed into the hotel, heading directly for the elevator.

When they reached their suites, Chastity's mouth dropped open. The suite was bigger than they had ever expected. It had a Jacuzzi, hot tub, an all-glass shower, bar, a super king-size bed that spun around, and a bunch of other shit.

"Do you like the room?" Keem asked her.

"This is so beautiful. I wish that we lived here so we could find a house with all of this in it. What are we going to do today, and who is Pedro? Why is he giving us the room?" she curiously asked Keem.

"Well, Pedro is my supplier and that's the real reason why we are here for two days. I'm going to need you to carry some work back to Philly for me. Is that okay with you?"

Chastity looked at him wondering why she had to carry it. He had seen that look before and reiterated on it. "I need you to do this so that we can have the things that you always wanted. This is more about your happiness than it is about mine. Everything I'm doing is for you, Chas!"

"But how will I get it back and where will you be?"

"I'll be with you the whole time. They will tape it to your body so that it won't come up on the x-ray monitors. If I do it, they might stop me; but since you're a girl, it will be easy for you to get through. So, will you do this for us, so that I can take care of you the way you like?" Keem said.

Chastity thought about it for a few minutes. She would do anything for him to make money that he used to shower her with gifts. If anything happens, she knew he would help her, so she agreed to do it.

"Okay, I'll do it for you," she said as she sat on the bed.

Keem walked over to her and sat down. He put his arm around her and gave her a kiss. "Is there anything that you would like to do while we're waiting to meet with Pedro?"

"Can we go to the beach and relax for a while? I want to make a sandcastle and get a tan," she said, taking her bikini out of her bag.

'Okay, let's go have some fun on the beach and then later on we can have fun in the hot tub."

"You are so nasty," she said, as she changed into her bikini and readied herself to hit the beach.

Hakeem called his boys and let them know what was going on. He gave them all the info that he knew so far and then hung up so that he could also get ready.

* * *

Back in Philly, Kita was at her boyfriend's house in West Philly. They had just finished having sex and she wondered why he hadn't bought her a car yet. He told her a while ago that she would have one soon, but she was still waiting.

"When are you going to get my car like you said you would?" she asked, putting on her thong.

"Here you go with that shit again. I don't have the money yet to get you a car. I can barely pay for mine with this nut-ass-job I'm at. You're just gonna have to be patient and wait until I get my income tax money," Keith said, as he got dressed to take her home.

"I'm tired of waiting on your sorry ass. You shouldn't have told me that if you couldn't do it. You can't even buy me a fucking used car. Why am I even with your sorry ass? Besides some good dick, you can't do shit for me."

Kita was tired of all the bullshit that he was telling her. She knew that she was getting under his skin, but she didn't care anymore. She was only using him because his mom was sick with cancer; and when she died, he would get all her insurance money. She just couldn't take his broke-ass anymore, that's why she was fucking niggas on the side for money.

"Well bitch, if you're so fucking tired of me then leave me the fuck alone. Matter of fact, get the fuck out of my house and walk aback to South Philly, you trifling-ass project trick" Keith said, tired of her shit.

"You better take me the fuck back home. You brought me all the way down here, so you're going to take me home or call me a fucking cab."

"If I have to tell you one more time to get the fuck out of my crib, I'm going to throw you out."

Kita sat down on the bed, folding her arms over her chest and stared at him. "I'm not going anywhere, so do what you gotta do."

Without warning, Keith grabbed her by her hair and dragged her towards the door. He opened the bedroom door and walked down the steps with her in tow.

"Get the fuck off me nigga before you die in this bitch. Let me go!"

"I told you to leave peacefully, but you wouldn't listen. Now I'm 'a teach you a lesson," Keith said.

Before he made it to the door, Kita scratched his eye. He smacked the shit out of her, sending her to the ground in pain.

"I'm 'a kill you, pussy," she said, as she reached in her purse and pulled out her mace. She sprayed the shit in his eyes, and then kicked him in his nuts.

Keith fell to the floor and screamed out in pain. She then took the lamp sitting on the table and smacked him in the head with it. He lay on the floor unconscious, as she went inside his pockets and took all the money he had.

She ran out the door before he woke up. She then walked over to 52nd and Market and took a taxi home. When she counted the money, she only had $232.

"Broke-ass nigga," she said, as she relaxed in the car on her way home.

* * *

Later that night Hakeem and Chastity were on their way to the club to meet Pedro. Chastity had on a black Maje skirt with a white Max Mara button-down shirt. The skirt made her look as if it was painted on her body. It was so short and tight, that if she moved the wrong way, you would see all her assets.

Keem wore a tight fitted t-shirt and a pair of cargo shorts. He really didn't want to stay long because he was trying to fuck Chastity again. He had his hand between her legs, rubbing on her pussy through the lace panties she wore.

They got to Club Bamboo, she fixed her clothes, and they stepped out of the limo and headed for the door. When they reached the two, seven-foot bouncers, Hakeem gave them his name and they escorted him to a VIP booth.

"Drinks are on the house, so enjoy yourself. I'll let Pedro know that you're here," one of them said, as at Chastity's big ass. A drink could be put on it if she bent over even slightly, that's how juiced that shit looked.

Once the bouncers left, Chastity sat down and waited for the waitress to bring her drink. She was too young to drink any liquor, so she got some Jamaican-Me-Happy. Rich Homie's *I Know You Feel Some Type of Way* was flowing through the speaker. Chastity started dancing in her sea, making her already too short skit rise up even more.

Hakeem sipped on rosé, as he watched the girls on the dance floor with barely anything on grinding on niggas and each other's. The place was jam-packed. Right next to them in the other VIP section was Yo Gotti, Rick Ross, and his team, as well as Floyd Mayweather.

Niggas were watching every chick in the building, trying to see whom they would be taking home tonight. Some of them were even watching Chastity.

"This club is really nice. Look at all these rappers over there. I didn't know that Miami would be this fun," she said.

"I'm glad that you're enjoying yourself. I'll be right back. I'm going to the bathroom," Keem said, as he made his way through the crowd.

Chastity was still dancing in her seat, taking cell-phone pictures of all the celebrities she saw. One dude walked up to her and sat down.

"What's up with you, sexy? Why are you over here by yourself?" he asked. His chain and watch had so much ice in it that it nearly blinded Chastity's eyes.

She smiled at him before saying, "I'm just waiting for my friend to return from the bathroom."

"Is he a friend or your man?"

Chastity thought about it for a minute because they never even established what their relationship was. The dude sensed her hesitation. "Well. Since you don't know yet, here is my number if you want to be with a real man who can take care of you," he said, taking her phone and storing his number in it.

He passed her phone back and stood up. "Your body is really putting that skirt to shame. A woman like you would make a nigga settle down for real. Just let me know when you're reading to step your game up."

He walked away without even telling her his name. Chastity was impressed. She looked at her phone and saw that a call had been made to somebody named Trillz. She didn't know who that was, so she decided to call the number back. Just as she was about to press redial, Keem walked up.

"You ready to head upstairs with me to meet Pedro?"

Chastity nodded and stood up to fixing her skirt, while taking Keem's hands. She followed him as the bouncer escorted them up a set of stairs and into an office right above the dance floor.

When they walked in, Pedro was sitting at his desk talking on his office phone. He motioned for them to sit down, while he finished the call. After a couple of minutes, he ended the call and stood to greet his visitors.

"Hello, my name is Pedro and welcome to Miami. I've heard that you are trying to become the next big thing out in Philly. I don't know if Chris told you, but there will be some very big shoes to fill. My partner, and owner of this club, retired from the game. He is now living life to the fullest and enjoying his money without a care in the world. He may briefly stop by tonight. If he does, I'll introduce you to him," he said, as he poured himself a drink.

"Would you like anything to drink?"

They both shook their heads declining and watched Pedro walk back to his seat. "Please excuse my manners, who is this lovely lady that you brought with you?"

"My name is Chastity," she said with a smile.

"It's nice to meet you, Chastity," he said and then kissed the back of her hand making her blush.

They talked for about 30 minutes, getting down to business, when a man walked into the office wearing a pair of True Religion jeans and white Polo shirt with a red logo on it.

He and Pedro embraced briefly before he turned and looked towards Chastity and Keem.

Chastity appeared dazed as she noticed how well built he was. His arms looked as if he had been working out forever. They bulged through his shirt.

"Chris told me that he sent new people out here, so I decided to stop in and check on you."

"Well, I'm fine. I was just talking to them. Hakeem and Chastity, I would like you to meet Chris' brother, and my partner, E.J."

Hakeem couldn't believe that he just said that name. He had heard so many rumors about him when he was doing his two years upstate at SCI-Pine Grove. Now he was in the same room as the legendary Eric Johnson. E.J. was the same person who locked down the East Coast and killed anybody in his way, even his own best friend.

Hakeem stood up and shook his hand.

"It's a pleasure to meet you, man. I heard some good things as well as some bad things about you. Just be careful and take your time, because you don't want to rush into anything. That can be your downfall." E.J. said, as he turned back towards his friend.

"Well, I'm going to get out of here now. I'll see you tomorrow so that we can go over the plans for the new club. You and your beautiful lady friend enjoy the rest of your stay here. If you need anything while you're here, just let one of the managers know and they will accommodate you as they see fit. Take it easy everybody," he said, giving Pedro another hug while whispering something in his ear. He then walked out of the office and into the crowd of partygoers.

While Pedro and Keem talked some more, Chastity watched the surveillance monitors, when she saw the man who just left the office leaving with the guy who came over to talk to her. They jumped in a drop-top Bentley GT that was parked in front of the club and pulled out. She knew right then that there were some rich niggas out here, and that's the life that she wanted.

* * *

The next day they were set to return to Philly. Pedro didn't want them to stay the extra day that he had planned.

Chastity had the six keys strapped to her body, while she wore a dress that made her look pregnant.

They walked nervously through the airport, as the TSA works and police watched for anything suspicious.

"It feels like they are looking at us. I'm getting scared," Chastity said, holding Keem's hand.

"We're almost on the plane. Stop bitching up on me. I thought you said you were a rider? Remember the number one rule: If we get caught, you don't know anything or anybody. Never be a snitch, because that will get you a one-way ticket to hell."

"I'm not worried about that. I will never tell. I just don't like how everybody keeps staring."

"Look how beautiful you are. They might think that you're some actress or something. They can look all they want, but don't touch because you're all mine," he said, kissing her cheek.

They made it onto the plane safely and sat in their seats. The whole plane ride back, Chastity was thinking about how it will feel to be living like a queen. Thanks to everyone around her, she was becoming street smart. She was learning too much, too fast, and soon everyone would feel the effects of her intelligence.

EIGHT

HAKEEM HAD BEEN BACK in Philly for about two hours. After he dropped off Chastity at home, he went to meet up with Chris at their usual spot.

When he pulled inside the Pathmark parking lot, Chris was already there waiting. He jumped out of the car and got in with Chris.

"I see you made it back safely. How was everything in beautiful Miami?"

"It was cool, and I met your brother while we were there. All this time I never knew that you were related," Keem said, passing him the bag with the work in it.

"That is because that information was on a need-to-know basis. When you needed to know, I would have told you," he said, with irritation covering his face.

He didn't want his brother to be out there giving up his identity to people he hardly knew. It's bad enough that everybody thought that he was dead. Hopefully this nigga doesn't run his mouth to anybody about it. If he does, he'll find himself sleeping with the fishes.

"I don't want you to say nothing to anybody about you meeting my brother. He's not in the game anymore and I don't need anybody trying to put his name back out there. Are we clear on this?"

"Crystal! You will never have to worry about that," Keem said,

"Good, now, let's get down to business so that you can get out of here and make some money."

Chris punched in some digits on the radio, flicked on his lights, and turned on the AC. The dashboard opened up on the

Cadi revealing one of the stash spots. He took out the digital scale and placed five of the six bricks inside.

Chris cut the brick in half and weighed it. Once he weighed out the half, he wrapped it up and slid it in the bag.

"That's a half a brick right there. Make sure that money comes back. Once you flip that, I'll hit you with something else. I'll have more product coming in next week. My other mules will be rotating every week. I'll let you know when we need you to take that trip again," Chris said, as he put the other half in the stash box with the rest and closed it up.

"Well, let me get out of here. I have money to get at right now and my boys are low. With this, we should be all the way straight until we re-up," Keem said as he exited the car.

Chris pulled off and headed for his stash spot. He was going to drop the work off to his girls and head home to his wife, Nyia. He kept the same girls Ed used before all that shit went down. Sharrell had to stop working for a while because she was pregnant. Once she gave birth, she would return. All and all, he had a reliable team that he trusted to run shit without him being there.

* * *

After Chastity settled in from her trip, she took a taxi over to Rudy's house so that they could catch up on everything from the last couple of days. Rudy told her over the phone about the dude she was messing with. She didn't tell her that she fucked both of them for the money. That was her business only.

"So you mean to tell me that he canceled y'all trip early because he wanted you to bring drugs back? That's fucking crazy, girl! He would be buying me all types of shit right now," Rudy said, as they sat in the living room.

"I thought he was taking me on a vacation, but he really was taking care of business. At first, I was mad but I still ended up having some fun. It was so beautiful down there. One day, I'm going to live there."

While they talked, Kita and Sharon walked in. They had several bags in their hands, so both Rudy and Chastity knew exactly where they were coming from.

"What's up bitches?" Kita said smiling, as she set bags down on the couch.

"Hey!" they said in union.

"How was your trip, Chas?" Did you see any fine-ass niggas out there?" Sharon asked, sitting next to her.

"It was nice, and there were too many niggas out there. I didn't pay them any attention though, because I was with my man."

"Girl, you better wise up and stop thinking that. That nigga is only fucking you. He's desperately trying to brainwash you so he can use you to his advantage. Look at you. You are the most beautiful girl I ever seen, and you're not even 18 yet. You look and are built as if you're over 21. You have to start taking advantage of those features. Real talk!" Kita said.

Chastity thought about it for a minute, but then thought that Kita was just jealous that she had Keem first.

"I know he's not doing anything, because he's with me whenever he ain't with his boys."

"Okay, if that's what you think. Well, we are about to go out to King of Prussia to grab some shit. Do y'all want to come?" Kita asked.

"How are we getting there, because that ride on SEPTA is too fucking long?" Rudy said.

Kita held up a set of car keys while smiling. "Some nigga I know let me hold his wheel."

"What kind of car does he have?" Chastity asked.

"A Chevy Tahoe?"

Damn, that ain't no car, that's a big-ass truck. We can get so much shit from there. I'm going, are you, Chas?" Rudy asked.

"Hell yeah, let's roll!"

They jumped in the truck and headed out to the mall to do what they did best. Chastity kept thinking about what Kita said. She didn't want anybody to take her man away from her because then she would probably be left with nothing again. She decided that she would do whatever she needed to do to keep him.

* * *

It was just getting dark outside and Hakeem was on his way out of the Wilson projects to meet some girl named Meka to cut up his heroin for him. She had been doing that for him for a while now. All she ever wanted was a couple of dollars and some dick here and there.

As he parked in front of her crib, he never noticed the two niggas that were creeping up to him in all black. They had hoodies on real tight around their faces.

When he stepped out of the car, he was met by a chrome 44 Bulldog that was aimed at his face.

"You know what this is, nigga? Give that work up, and don't do anything stupid or your brains will be all over the ground," one stick-up kid said.

The whole time that Keem had been hustling, he never had a gun pointed at him except for when the cops locked him up. This shit right here infuriated him to the point where he wanted to try his hand, but he knew that would only lead to his demise.

He didn't want to give up Chris' work, but his hands were tied. He passed the two stick-up kids the bag with the dope in it and put his hands up in the air.

"Where's the money at too, nigga? Don't fucking play with me. I'm not in the mood."

"All I have is the work. I just gave all my money up when I went to re-up."

The other dude checked his pockets and only found $200. He took that from him, along with this car keys. He put the money in the bag and tossed the car keys down the street, as they ran off around the corner.

"Damn, man. What the fuck am I gonna do?"

* * *

Chastity came in the house around 10:00 and went upstairs to put away the clothes that she purchased. They had hit Victoria Secret, the Polo Store, and Forever 21 for almost $1,500 apiece. Most of the stuff she let Rudy take home with her, so Keem wouldn't see it. When he gave her more money to buy shit with, she would pocket it and go get her stuff from there.

She only came home with the stuff from Victoria Secret. She was going to wear something sexy for him tonight. After she put the stuff up, she went downstairs and heard him in the basement talking to Reese and Mal.

"I'm fucking dead if I don't find a way to get this money back. He will never believe that me that somebody stuck me up an hour or so after I left him," Keem said to his friends.

"You don't have any idea who could have done it?" Reese asked.

Keem shook his head no, as he paced back and forth trying to figure this shit out.

"I hope that bitch you be fucking and getting to cut that shit up didn't have anything to do with this. After all, you were in front of her crib when it happened," Mal said.

"I wasn't fucking her, man, she was just taking care of the work for me," Keem said, putting a finger to his mouth ad point upstairs.

59

They both caught on quick to what he meant. He knew that Chastity had just walked in the house, so just in case she was listening, she wouldn't get mad.

"We are going to have to do something about this man, because I'm not going to be able to keep him from asking for his money. Thank goodness that I only have about a week to do this," Keem said.

Reese looked at him. "*We* only have a week?"

"Right, we're a team so let's get this shit together," Mal said, looking at his friends.

"How about we find a couple of niggas, set them up, and rob them," Keem said.

"We are going to need someone to get close to them without setting off any alarms," Mal said.

"I'll sleep on it and get back to y'all in the morning. I'll figure something out," Keem said, as they headed upstairs.

Chastity ran back upstairs so they wouldn't see her. She heard their whole conversation and she knew that her man was in some trouble. She didn't want anything to happen to him, so she hoped that he would be able to rectify the problem before she lost him.

She went in their room and sat down on the bed. Her phone rang. When she looked at the screen, she saw that it was Rudy.

"Hello."

"Hey, girl. I was just calling you to let you know we're home. We're going to the Level Room on Friday, so make sure that you're free. It's going to be girls' night out. I'll see you tomorrow when y'all pick me up from school."

"Okay, we'll talk tomorrow, 'cause I have something to tell you but not over the phone" Chastity said, as Keem walked into the room.

"Alright, see you then, and don't be doing no freaky shit to make you get up late."

"Bye, bitch," Chastity said, ending the call.

Keem walked over to her and sat down next to her on the bed. He began taking his clothes off, while deep in thought.

"What's wrong?"

"Nothing, a couple of niggas robbed me taking all of the work that I just came back with," he said, holding his head down.

Keem didn't tell her that they only took half of a brick because he was hoping that he could get her to feel sorry for him. While he was downstairs, he figured out a way to set some niggas up. Every nigga loves some good pussy from a beautiful woman. Chastity had the looks and the body of a goddess. He knew that if he could get her to help him out, he would get that money--plus some. He just had to play his cards right.

"Oh my God! So what are you going to do?" she asked.

"I don't know yet, but if I don't get his money by the end of the week, he might try to kill me."

Chastity put her arms around his neck, straddling him. "How can I help? I'll do anything you need me to do."

That's what he needed to hear, but he had to make sure that she would really do it.

"Thanks, but I can't put you in that kind of danger for what I'm about to do."

"You're not putting me in danger, Hakeem. I told you that I would do anything for you, and I meant that. So tell me what you need me to do."

"Well, I'm gonna have to go out and rob a few eats. I need a chick to help me set them up. It will only take a few minutes to do it and we'll be in and out within a few minutes."

He looked at her and saw that he had her, so he told her the whole plan, and her role would be. Afterwards, she agreed to do it until they got all of his connects money back.

Keem knew that it would only take maybe one lick to get the 30 grand for Chris. That's why he told her that they took it all, so that he could really make a come-up off of it.

"You won't let anything happen to me, right?" she asked, holding him.

"Never," he said, as he rubbed her ass through the PZI jeans that she was wearing.

Chastity began rocking back and forth on him as they kissed each other.

She got up and started unbuttoning his jeans, and pulling them off... with his boxers following. Next, she got on her knees in front of the bed, rubbing his dick up and down. Once she had him hard, she put his dick in her mouth and started moving her head up and down.

This was Chastity's third time giving Keem head. She had been practicing on Kita's dildos, with Rudy and Sharon showing her how to do it. When she was home by herself, she would watch Superhead's sex tapes so she could become the best at what she was doing.

The first time was bad; but the second time, she made the nigga's toes curl. This time, though, she was determined to make him blow a gasket.

"Damn, baby, that shit feels so fucking good," Keem moaned, as he lay back on the bed.

Chastity took his dick out of her mouth and then began licking up and down his shaft. She took his balls into her mouth and started sucking on them until his toes started to wiggle.

She then spit all over his dick and started licking the head with her tongue, before taking him in her mouth again and then pulling out.

"Oh shit, Chas, what are you doing to me?" Keem asked, as he gripped the sheets on the bed.

He squirmed, trying to get away from her vicious blowjob, but she wouldn't let him.

"Don't run now, nigga," she said, playfully trying to hold onto his legs.

Keem couldn't take it any longer and shot his entire load in her mouth.

She looked at him and laughed because he was acting as if he was asleep now.

"So you want to play sleep now? I guess I'm going to have to wake you back up."

Chastity stood up and removed all of her clothes, showcasing her perfect body. The tan that she received while in Miami made her look as if she was no longer white. Now she looked like a true African American.

She crawled up on him, reached up underneath her, and stuck his still hard dick inside her wet pussy. She then bent down and whispered in his ear, "I'm 'a fuck the shit out of you tonight."

Hakeem opened his eyes and smiled at her, grabbing her ass and squeezing it.

"Not if I don't beat this pussy up first."

Chastity started sliding up and down on his dick, trying to match his rhythm. She leaned back, putting her hands on his legs, and started working the shit out of her pussy muscles, just as she had seen on the videos and when she and Rudy watched Sharon and Kita.

They fucked until her pussy cried out in orgasm after orgasm. She slid off of his limp dick and lay down next to him, with her head on his chest.

"Are you tired?" he asked, stroking her hair.

"Yes, I am."

"Good, 'cause I'm not done yet."

Hakeem rolled over and got on top of Chastity. He kissed her body all the way down to her feet. He worked his way back up, stopping at her clit.

He began kissing it. He then flicked his tongue near the opening of her ass, licking all around it. He dipped his tongue inside, while playing with her clit with two fingers.

Chastity opened her legs wider and reached for his head, pushing him further inside. He sucked every inch of her ass and pussy, then around her pussy lips.

"Oh, my God, baby, please no more. I can't take it!" Chastity screamed out, as she came close to an electrifying orgasm.

Keem started tongue fucking her, until she shot all in his mouth. When her body finished convulsing, he slid up her body and kissed her passionately, tasting each other's bodily fluids.

They lay cuddled up for a few, before drifting off into a deep sleep.

* * *

The next day at school, Chastity and Rudy sat at the lunch table talking about what happened to Keem yesterday. Rudy said people had seen the dudes run away, but they didn't know whom they were.

Chastity told her what she and Hakeem were planning to do to get the money back.

"Girl, you better be careful, 'cause these niggas don't care who they kill out there," Rudy said, eating her fries.

"I know! He said that when it's time to go down, he and his boys will be there to make sure nothing happens to me. Besides, the dude will think I'm the victim too, Hakeem told me."

"Okay, y'all seem like y'all have it all figured out. Still be real careful, because I don't want you to get hurt. You're my best friend."

They shared a hug before getting up and heading to their next classes. Before she could walk into her history class, her phone began vibrating. It was Keem, so she went into the ladies room to answer it.

"Hey, baby, what's up? I was just heading to my history class. Is everything okay?"

"Yeah, I'm good. I have a potential for us, and we can hit him tonight. I'll give you all the details when you get out of school today."

"Okay, I'll see you later then."

"I love you, girl," Keem said, before hanging up.

That caught Chastity off guard, as she looked at her phone. She couldn't believe that he just said that. She never imagined hearing those words from anybody but her grandma and best friend. Chastity smiled as she headed back to class.

* * *

Later that night, out in west Oak Lawn, Chastity and Hakeem sat in his car. Reese and Mal were already in the bar on Church Street. They were about to rob some nigga named Ralph, who lived a couple blocks away.

Mal used to fuck his sister, so he knew that he was a big-time drug dealer up north. Now they were going to take whatever he had in his crib. First, they had to get him there, and that's where Chastity came into play. She was supposed to flirt with him and convince him to take her to his crib.

Keem knew he wouldn't turn her down, because she was a badass bitch, plus she had on her freakin' dress. It was a black Prada dress that came off her shoulders and was just low enough to cover her ass. If she bent down for anything, you could get a glimpse of all her ass and thong.

"Now you know what to do, right? Don't worry, Reese and Mal will be watching you the whole time, and I'll be right here when you come out."

"I'm not scared," she lied. She had been nervous ever since they left the house. She just hoped that everything went according to the plan so she could return home.

She stepped out of the car, fixed herself, and then walked inside the bar. Beyoncé's *Dance for You* was playing on the jukebox, while a couple of girls were on the dance floor winding to the beat.

Chastity walked over to a booth and took a seat. Every nigga in there was watching her ass as she sat down.

"What can I get you to drink?" the bartender asked.

"Um, let me get a shot of Moscato."

Chastity was too young to drink, but she had to get something so that it would calm her nerves. She noticed all the attention she was getting and grew even more nervous. When the bartender came back with her drink, she went into her purse to pay for it, but he stopped her.

"The man over there already paid for it," he said, pointing to the guy at the end of the counter.

"Tell him I said thank you."

The waiter nodded his head and walked off as Chastity took a sip of the drink. It was a little sweet, so she drank some more. It made her feel more comfortable.

A couple of minutes later, the guy who sat at the end walked up to her. "Hello, beautiful, my name is Ralph. What's yours?"

She smiled and said her name. She was surprised at how cute he was. He had long braids and a beard that let her know he was Muslim.

They talked for about five minutes, and he already asked her to come back to his place.

She had to play her role so she said, "What's in it for me if I go back to your place?"

"You'll see! So are you coming? My car is right outside."

"Well, let's get out of here then," she said, as they headed for the door.

When they got into his Lexus, Mal and Reese jumped in the car with Keem and they followed him.

Ralph put his hand on Chastity's lap, making her jump. "I'm not going to hurt you. I just wanted to cop a feel," he said smiling.

She was feeling tipsy just from that one drink. She smiled back and took his hand, placing it between her legs. He started rubbing her pussy and she started getting wet.

As soon as they pulled in his driveway, they stepped out of the car. Chastity pulled her dress down some and started following him to the door. When he opened the door, three guns were in his face.

"Say anything and I'll blow your fucking head off. Get the fuck in the house," the masked man said, as the other two followed behind them.

He pushed him on the couch. "Take the bitch outside and body her ass. Put her in the trunk afterwards."

"Wait, man, you don't have to do this. I can pay you whatever you want. I have a family, man. I'm not trying to die," Ralph said in a bitching manner.

"So why would you bring a piece of pussy to the place where your family rests their heads? I hope it was worth it," he said, as Ralph led him to the safe.

When he opened the safe, Hakeem smacked him with the butt of the gun twice, knocking him unconscious. He began loading up three pillowcases full of money, which he then took downstairs where Reese was waiting.

Mal had pretended to take Chastity outside and kill her, but they were sitting in the car waiting. Keem didn't want her in there just in case she had to see a murder. Since Ralph bitched up so easy, that made the shit go smoother than he expected.

What they didn't know was that was only change compared to what he had in the other bedroom. They left without ever having the chance to discover it.

When they got in the car, Hakeem pulled off his mask and gave Chastity a kiss. "Good job, baby!"

They hit the road heading back home to count the money that they made in less than an hour.

NINE

TWO WEEKS LATER, CHASTITY was sitting on the bed, butt naked, counting money that they had gotten from their last mark. All together, they had robbed six people.

"There is only $17,825 here. Is that all we got this time?"

"Yeah, and we still have to split it down with Reese and Mal. So start taking your money out now. You get a grand, and put the rest in the bag. I'm going to go take a shower," Keem said, heading for the bathroom.

They had just finished having sex and then started counting the money. She got off the bed and put her money in the drawer. She didn't know that Hakeem was getting over on her. She thought he was paying back this big bill he owed to the connect. But he, Reese, and Mal were actually pocketing the money. Altogether, they made over $60,000 and after paying Chris his 30 stacks, they each had a little over 10 stacks. Chastity came out of the deal with around $4,000.

Ring, ring, ring, the doorbell cried out. Chastity grabbed her robe and went to answer the door. When she opened it, Reese was standing there.

"Hey Reese, come on in. Keem is in the shower. He should be out in a few minutes."

Reese watched Chastity's ass as she walked towards the steps. He could tell she wasn't wearing anything under her robe because it jiggled with every step she took. His suspicions were confirmed when she started walking up the steps, and he saw nothing but the back of her light-skinned ass. For a moment, he thought she did that on purpose, but then he realized that her robe was too small. Whatever the case may be, she made his dick grow unusually hard. He went to the basement to wait for Keem.

Chastity went back in the room so she could ready to shower, when she noticed Keem's phone flashing. She walked over and looked at the screen. Curiosity got the best of her, when she saw that he had four missed text messages.

She checked the first one that was from some girl named Meka. It read:

Meka: Hey baby, I miss you so much SMH. When can a bitch get some more of that good dick? Call me! TTYL. xoxo

The second and third texts were from Reese and Mal telling him that they would be over soon.

The fourth text was what really got her attention. It was from Chris

Chris: Yo, hit me up. I got that $30K. Your bill is paid, Let me know if you want to grab another half one.

All this time he was lying to her to get her help in setting up niggas. She thought it was to pay Chris back, but they were keeping all the money, giving her chump change. Then on top of that, he was fucking some bitch named Meka. Chastity was mad, but she decided not to say anything right then. When the time was right, she was going to address it.

Keem came out of the bathroom and began dressing. Chastity left the room with her clothes so she could get dressed in the bathroom. She and Rudy were supposed to get their permits today. She wasn't worried about him catching her reading his text messages because she had erased them all.

* * *

Chastity and Rudy both passed their written tests on the first try. They scheduled the driving part for the weekend, and then left the DMV with permits in their hands and smiles on their faces.

"I can't wait to save my money and get a car. Watch how many bitches be hating on us," Rudy said, as they sat in the taxi on their way home.

"Well if I get a car, you know that you can drive it whenever you want. Are Kita and Sharon still going to Club Onyx tonight?"

"Hell yeah, them bitches going. I want to go too, but I'm going to need some I.D. If that girl that be with Kita don't go, she said I could use hers. We both look as if we could bet twins."

"Well, none of the people I know look like me. I guess that I won't be going with y'all."

"If you're not going, then either am I. We can find something else to get into. How about we go chill at my friend's crib for a while? I want to hit him up for some money. We won't be there too long, okay?" Rudy said, as they stepped out of the taxi.

Her friend, Budda, lived on the next terrace from her, so they cut through the little pathway to get to his crib. Rudy had called him already, so he was standing in the door waiting.

"What's up, Shorty?" Who is this with you looking all sexy?" Budda asked, stepping to the side allowing them in.

"This is my best friend, Chastity. Chastity, this is Budda. Don't pay him any attention, he always acts stupid."

Budda watched Chastity walk and her ass was all he kept staring at as it swayed side to side in that sweat suit.

They all sat on the couch as Budda sparked up the dutch sitting on the table.

"You smoke, Chastity?"

She shook her head that she didn't, as Rudy stuck her hand out grabbing it from him and taking a couple of puffs.

"So what brings you over here this early? I usually don't hear from you until after 9:00 at night," Budda said, sitting back on the couch.

"I came here because I need a couple of dollars. Chastity and I just passed our permit test and I'm trying to celebrate tonight with my friends at my crib. Since we were supposed to hook up tonight, I thought I'd come over now. Is that okay with you?" Rudy asked him.

Budda took a couple more pulls of the dutch, before passing it back to Rudy.

"It's okay but my lil' sister is in the room with a couple of her friends, and my cousin is in there with some chick," he said, pointing to his room.

"Oh, well I guess I'll have to hook you up tomorrow then."

"How much did you need?"

"Let me get $50. I'll call you tonight after my friends leave; and if you're not busy, you can come over," Rudy said, putting out the dutch.

He got up and walked into the kitchen. "Come here for a minute, Rudy."

She got up off the couch and walked in the kitchen to see what Budda wanted.

Chastity watched *The Jerry Springer Show* on TV, while she looked at her Instagram pictures that she added this morning.

She heard a soft moan coming from the kitchen, so she got up to make sure her friend was okay. When she looked in there, Rudy was laying with her back on the table, while Budda ate her pussy. Chastity shook her head as she watched her friend enjoying herself.

She went and sat back down on the couch. Five minutes later, they came out of the kitchen, and sat back on the couch with Chastity. Rudy winked at Chastity, as they watched *Jerry* until it was over.

They left his house and Chastity burst out laughing. "Girl, you are so fucking crazy. On the kitchen table, though?"

"Shit! He asked, and since he paid for it, I let him," Rudy said, holding up the money.

"Why do you have sex for money though when you can get a job?"

"Girl, we are only 16, still in high school, and don't have working papers. Who the hell is going to hire us? My sister said that no white man is going to hire a young, black girl that don't have any type of job training. That's why I don't."

Chastity could understand that and decided to leave it alone for now. She was experiencing a lot to be so young. One thing that she did know was that which doesn't kill you would only make you stronger.

"Well, when I start making a lot of money, you can come and ask me for some; and I'll give your ass more than what they're giving you," Chastity said.

"Wait, girl, I don't know what you heard, but I'm strictly dickly," Rudy said laughing.

Chastity started laughing, too. "Shut up, you know what I mean. You're my best friend, so what I have, you have. As a matter of fact, I have some money at home that Keem gave me, so I'll pay for our get together tonight."

"That's cool, but where are we going to get our drinks from? Kita and Sharon might not be home before the store closes," Rudy said.

"Well, since I don't drink, I'll leave that up to you."

Chastity only had one drink before, and that was during her robbery with Keem. She liked the way the drink made her feel, but she never had any more.

"I know a couple of people, so you're right, I'll take care of it. Now, let's go see what we're going to wear."

They made their way up to Rudy's room where Chastity still had some of her clothes, and they picked out a couple of outfits to wear. She was starting to get accustomed to living the glamorous life, and whatever she wanted, Keem made sure she got it. That's why she didn't want to lose her man, so she pretended not to know about his other chick. Even though he told her he loved her, and she was living with him, she still was jealous. She decided when the time was right; she was going to give him a banging surprise.

TEN

HAKEEM HAD JUST LEFT his meeting with Chris, picking up additional work ever since they had been robbing niggas all over Philly; he was able to pay for it up front, instead of getting it on consignment. He kept all of his money at Reese's crib so that Chastity didn't know how much he actually had.

Hakeem, Reese, and Mal were each sitting on around $60,000 apiece, but he only kept $10,000 around at a time for Chastity to see. He had already passed the chop shop on 52nd and Wynfield to pay for the Audi 8 that he was gathering the paperwork ready for. He told them that he would pick it up later that day. It only cost him $7,000 and he added $2,000 more for the rims that came off of another vehicle.

He was riding down 23rd Street on his way to drop the work off to Reese, when he noticed a state trooper driving behind him.

Ever since the murder rate had been going up every year, the mayor had assigned state troopers to patrol the streets periodically strictly for guns. They would pull over people, search their car, and then let them go without even giving them a ticket.

Hakeem already knew the deal, so when the trooper's light came on, he pulled over. "Damn, a couple more blocks and I would have been at Reese's crib," he said to himself.

They were on 23rd and Dickerson on the corner right next to the poppy store. The troopers got out of the patrol car and walked up to Keem's car.

"How are you doing today, sir? We pulled you over because your taillights are out. Can I please see your license, registration, and proof of insurance?"

Hakeem gathered all the paperwork and presented it to the state trooper.

A marked police car passed by when they stopped to check on the troopers. It was a K-9 unit, and when the dog started barking, they all looked at one another. The officer pulled over and led the dog out from the back.

Hakeem became nervous when they ordered him to exit the vehicle. He knew if they found the half a key, he would be going to jail for a long time.

"What is this about? I haven't done anything wrong," he said, as he opened the door.

"We need to search your car to make sure there are no weapons inside," one trooper said, as he frisked Hakeem.

"I don't have anything in my car that would get me in trouble. I just dropped off my mom at the market, and was on my way home to grab her coupons," Keem said, trying to get off out of this before they found the drugs in the backseat, under the headrest.

The dog began barking more intensely when they opened the backdoor. The officers started searching the car, but were unable to find anything. Hakeem thought he was in the clear until one of the state troopers felt how lose the headrest was and removed it.

When he felt inside the seat, he pulled out a 9mm semi-automatic and a plastic bag that had something wrapped inside. He held it up to the other officers smiling.

"You have the right to remain silent. Anything you say can and will be used against you...," the trooper said, cuffing Hakeem while continuing to read him his rights.

Hakeem shook his head because he knew he was done, plus he was still on state parole. Even if he was awarded bail, they were going to hold him on a detainer until the outcome of his case.

* * *

Chastity was at Rudy's house enjoying the little get-together they were having. Of the 10 people at the party, only two were boys. One was Neatra's friend, and he brought his 13-year-old cousin with him who he was watching him because his aunt had to make a run.

Besides Rudy and Neatra, Chastity had only seen the other five girls around school. Everyone sat around the table about to play pitty-pat for shots. At first, Chastity didn't want to play because she didn't drink, but Rudy talked her into it.

They had all types of drinks from Hennessy to Grey Goose; each of them put a glass in front of them as some girl named Nay Nay dealt the cads. Nobody knew what the drink in front of them was because they had the 13-year-old pour all of them since he couldn't participate.

"Okay, everybody knows the rules. Whoever wins the hand, the rest of us have to drink what's in the glass. Okay, Nique, it's your pluck," Nay Nay said, looking at her cards.

"Deuces are wild, right?" she asked.

"Yeah! How many times are we going to say it?" Neatra said, smacking her teeth.

Nique laid her hand down because she had three deuces in her hand. Everybody sighed, as they gulped down their drinks.

For the next 30 minutes, everyone took turns winning the game, while the losers had to drink more and more liquor. When they grew tired of playing cars, and everyone was tipsy, they went into the living room to play truth or dare.

Chastity was feeling surprisingly nice from the three glasses she had. She didn't know what she had, but she was damn sure wanted some more. She realized that drinking wasn't all that bad.

"I'll go first," Neatra said, spinning the bottle.

It landed on Leana. She sat there for a minute before saying, "I'll take truth."

"Neatra was trying to figure out some of the dirt she heard about her friend. "Is it true that you gave some dude on the basketball team a blow job under the bleachers?"

"True! My turn to spin!" Leana said, as if she didn't even care. She spun the bottle, and it landed on Tanya.

"Hmmm, let me see. I'm going to take the truth."

"Is it true that you like eating girl's pussies while their boyfriends watch?" Leana asked.

"No, I never did that before," she said, trying not to appear embarrassed.

"You're lying, girl, because I heard that and I saw you do it with my own eyes," Neatra said, standing up.

Tanya looked at her puzzled, so Neatra gladly refreshed her memory. "I came to pick up my money from your cousin, when we heard a voice in her room. We looked in there and you were eating Syida's coochie while her dude watched by the bed. Now do you remember?"

Now with embarrassment covering her face, she said, "Yes, it's true."

So that she didn't feel bad, Neatra said, "Don't worry, girl, we all tried it before. Some of us like to get it, and some like to give it."

Everybody started laughing and then Tanya spun the bottle. It stopped on the quiet girl that had been looking at Chastity all night.

"Truth or dare, Meka?"

"That name caught Chastity's attention. When she tried to put a face to the name, they both stared at each other.

Meka wasn't ugly at all. She was brown-skinned, with short hair, real big tittles, and a skinny body that didn't go with her long legs. She looked as if she was six feet tall.

After the staredown, because they knew whom each other were, Meka said, "Truth."

"Is it true that you're sleeping with someone's man in here?" Tanya asked, because she also knew.

Meka looked at Chastity again, and said, "Fuck it, I've slept with all of y'all niggas in here. They paid for it, so I put it on them."

Everyone appeared shocked at how bold she was. The only person in the room had a serious boyfriend, and that was Chastity. Rudy shook her head at Chastity's, telling her no.

Chastity wasn't about to do anything to the girl. Since the nigga that came over was Meka's boyfriend, she decided to get even. She instead waited for the right time.

Meka spun the bottle and it landed on Rudy. "Dare," Rudy said confidently.

"I dare you and Chastity to make out with each other," Meka said.

Rudy and Chastity looked at Meka as if she lost her mind. Just then, Chastity's cell phone rang. She looked at the screen, but didn't recognize the number.

"Hello."

"Baby, this is Keem. I've just gotten locked up, and I'm waiting to see a judge to get bail. I need you to get me out of here before they drop a detainer on me."

"Oh my God!" Chastity said, as tears began to well up in her eyes. She stood to her feet and walked into the kitchen. "What am I supposed to do when they give you bail? I can't come up there. I'm not old enough."

"Get Kita or Sharon to do it. You're gonna have to give them the money to post my bail though. I'll give it back to you when I get out of here. I have to go now, but I'll call when I see the judge," he said, before hanging up.

Chastity didn't even get a change to find out what exactly he was in there for. She had just seen him earlier and now he was in jail.

Rudy walked in after she hung up. "What's wrong, Chas?"

"Hakeem is in jail, and he wants me to get Kita or Sharon to get him out when they give him bail."

"How much is it, because you know they will want that money back from him?"

"I don't know yet, but I'll give them the money. I have to go home so that I can be ready when he calls. Can you tell Kita to come to my house when she gets home?"

"I'll call her on our way to your house. I'm coming with you," Rudy said, and then called for a cab.

* * *

Two weeks had passed since the arrest of Hakeem. As he suspected, once he was processed, his parole officer dropped a detainer on him. Now he had to hope that he would be able to beat his case to return home. That seemed unlikely though because they found half a key and a gun in his car at the time of his arrest. He was facing some time if found guilty.

He told Chastity on the phone, "I need you to ask Kita to take you to pick up my car from Sam. Look in my black book bag for the address to the shop."

Hakeem didn't want to say the name of the chop shop over the phone, so he just told her where to look.

"When will you be coming home?"

"I'm 'a be real with you, Chas. I might not be coming home for a long time. They got me red-handed with something. What you can do is pick up that money from Reese for me. Tell him I said to give it to you."

"I wish I could come visit you, but they won't let me in without somebody 18 or older."

"That's okay. Whenever you can come, just do so. You have plenty of money to pay the bills. The 10 that's in the bag, give it to my lawyer for me. The money that you get from Reese is yours."

Tears filled Chastity's eyes at first, but then she thought about Meka not getting a dime of the money or being able to cheat with him for a while, and she quickly wiped the tears away.

"You have one minute remaining on this call," the operator said.

"I'll see if Kita will bring me up there next week. I just want to see you."

"Okay, but what do you have on right now?" Keem asked, being flirtatious.

"My shorts and shirt, why?"

"Keep that thing ti-," he said, before the phone was disconnected. Keem was mad because he couldn't finish his statement.

Chastity stripped down and then went in the bathroom to take a shower. After she finished getting dressed, she headed downstairs to make something to eat before she headed to see the lawyer. She called Kita after she took her shower and asked if she could take her to give the lawyer the money that Keem had told her about.

Once Kita arrived, they headed out to see the lawyer. Afterwards, they returned to the house so that Chastity could figure out what she was going to do about living there alone. It was time for her to step up and become head of the household. She didn't have a man there to take care of everything anymore.

ELEVEN

IT HAD BEEN A month now that Chastity had lived on her own. She convinced Rudy to stay with her some nights, and other nights she would stay over at her house. She hated being in the house alone without anybody there to hold her at night.

Hakeem tried to convince her to have phone sex with him but she couldn't get into it. She needed the real thing; however, it was currently locked away in a cage. Chastity really started to enjoy having sex. Keem had taught her a lot about it, although she really got her moves and tricks from her best friend and her sisters.

Every night that Chastity and Hakeem had sex, she would have him running from her vicious head game. Chastity became a pro at giving oral sex to her man. Now that he wasn't there, she began to pleasure herself.

She was in the bed talking to Rudy about not going to school the following day because she had to go see about the car that she was supposed to have gotten already. Sam had called her earlier and told her to pick it up in the morning. Kita had given her and Rudy driving lessons, and they both passed the driving test on their first try.

"So what are we going to do when we get your car tomorrow? Can we go for a long-ass drive and stunt on these bitches?" Rudy asked.

"Yeah, but we have to go pass the lawyer's office first and see what he found out about Hakeem's case."

'Well, I'm with you. Fuck that school shit anyway. I didn't want to go anyways."

"What time will you be here in the morning?"

"I'll be there around 9:00. That way we can get something to eat before we go."

Chastity hung up with Rudy and took a shower before laying down to watch TV. She started channel surfing when she ran across a soft porn movie by Zane.

It was about a stripper who was being real friendly with a bunch of men. She decided to watch to see what it was really about. As she watched, she felt herself getting turned on since Keem wasn't there to fulfill her desires; so she decided to take care of it herself.

Chastity removed her panties and began fingering her pussy as she watched the movie., She closed her eyes and started flicking her clit faster, imagining that it was Keem's tongue.

Just as she was ready to release, someone rang the doorbell. She looked at the clock and saw that it was 12:45 a.m. She wondered who the hell was at her door so late. When she looked out the window, she saw that it was Reese standing there.

She had been trying to get in touch with him since Hakeem told her to get the money. "Hold on, Reese."

She threw on her shorts and went downstairs to answer the door. When she opened the door, Reese walked in and went straight to the basement.

Chastity wondered what he was doing, so she headed down there to find out.

"Reese, what are you doing, and what's all that in that plastic?"

Reese looked up at her on the bottoms step. "I'm just getting the rest of the work so that I can knock it off. How is Keem doing behind those walls?"

"He's okay. I talked to him earlier today. Did you bring the money that he asked me to get from you? I need it so I can pay his lawyer some more, and the bills are due. I used the money we had here to put the down payment on him."

"That's why I came to get this work. I'll have it for you in a couple of days. I need to off this, and once it's gone you'll have the money."

"Okay, show yourself out when you're done," Chastity said, about to walk back upstairs.

"Hold on, I'm done now," he said, walking behind her.

Reese once again found himself looking at Chastity's ass as he followed her up the steps. Her shorts were tight and small, with half of her cheeks hanging out.

When they left the living room, Reese grabbed Chastity's arm, turning her around.

"I don't want you to take this the wrong way, but if you ever need me for anything, and I do mean anything, just remember that I'm only a phone call away."

"All I need is the money that you owe Keem. Can you make sure that I get it ASAP?"

Reese reached into his pocket and pulled out a knot of cash. He pulled off a couple of hundred dollar bills.

"I'll give you this right now if you let me taste that for a couple of minutes," he said, licking his lips.

Chastity couldn't believe she heard him correct. "What did you just say?"

"I said that I know you're lonely right now, and I'm just trying to taste that sweet pussy real quick. You are too beautiful to be here without a man to satisfy your needs."

"I'm good, thank you though. Now can you please leave so I can go to bed? As soon as you get Keem's money, can you bring it to me?"

Reese headed for the door, but then turned around. "Just don't forget what I told you. *Anything* you need."

He left and Chastity locked the door behind him. She couldn't wait to talk to Keem and let him know what he said to her. Something wasn't adding up with him, and she needed to find out.

Rudy and Chastity walked into the lawyer's office on JFK Boulevard. She walked up to the receptionist desk and waited for her to finish her call.

"How can I help you?" she asked, hanging up.

"Yes, I'm here to see Mr. Wimberly," Chastity said.

"Um, don't you mean Ms. Wimberly?" the receptionist said.

Chastity thought she was coming to see a man, but instead it was a woman. She could have sworn Hakeem said "him" when they talked on the phone.

"I'm sorry, this is my first time coming here, so I didn't know who it was," Chastity told her.

The lady paged someone, and three minutes later, a pretty light-skinned woman walked out. She was a bit skinny and she wore heels that made her look taller than she actually was.

"Hello ladies. My name is Lisa. Would you please follow me into my office so we can talk?"

They went into Lisa's office and took a seat. "I'm glad that you were finally able to get here. I want to first say that I'm sorry about your boyfriend. I have reviewed all the evidence that they have on him and I wouldn't feel right taking your money. This case is an open and shut case."

"Why do you say that? What does that even mean?" Chastity demanded.

"That means they will not hesitate to go to trial if he doesn't take a plea offer. We are still in the preliminary stages, but they are going to ask for at least 20 years. You have to understand the magnitude of this situation. He was caught with 504 grams of heroin and a weapon that he should not have had because he had a prior felony. The only thing that I will be able to do is get a good plea. If he goes to trial, he will be looking at 40 years. I talked to him and he wants to go all the way. I'll do everything in my power to beat it if you like," Lisa said.

"How much will it cost for all that?"

"You already gave me $10,000. If we go to trial, I'll need another $30,000."

"I'll have the money for you soon," Chastity said, as they left the office and went to pick up the car.

* * *

Later that night, Chastity was laying down on the bed trying to figure out how she was going to get the money to pay for Hakeem's lawyer. She had just talked to him on the phone. She told him how Reese was acting and about the proposition that he made her.

Hakeem was livid, but he tried not to show it. He instructed her to do whatever she could as long as it didn't interfere with the bills.

Chastity had counted the money that she had left from the robberies and the money that she tucked away whenever Keem gave her some. In total, she only had $5,000, which wasn't even close to what she needed.

She picked up Keem's phone earlier that day after she got his Audi 8 from the chop shop. She wanted to call his connect and get the money from him, but she was too scared. Chastity even thought about selling the car, but she knew that it would come in handy for when she had to get around.

Her mind was racing because so much was happening, and there was nothing she could do. She wanted her man home, but how would she with Reese refusing to give up Keem's money. She drifted off to sleep hoping that something good would eventually happen for her again. It seemed everyone who was good to her was taken out of her life. Now, once again, she was alone.

TWELVE

TWO MONTHS LATER, CHASTITY had just left her house and she was on her way to pick up Rudy when she saw Reese talking to a girl on the corner of 27th and Tasker. She hadn't heard from him in over a month. Every time she tried to call him about the money, he would say it was slow out or the workers had just been robbed. She had given up on him. When she saw him, she decided to try one more time, and if he didn't want to give it up, then fuck it.

Chastity parked and jumped out of the car wearing a sky-blue tennis skirt, a white short-sleeve Polo shirts and a pair of all-white Prada sneakers.

Reese saw the look on her face and excused himself from the girl he was talking to. He walked over to Chastity nonchalantly as if there was no beef between them.

"I was just trying to find out if you have the money for me so that I can pay Hakeem's lawyer."

"Don't worry about that. Me and Mal paid her last week, so it's taken care of," Reese said.

"That's funny because she called me this morning asking about her payment. So obviously she never received it or you're lying."

"I'll find out from Mal what happened and I'll let you know later on today," he said, turning to go finish his conversation with the female.

"Don't worry about it. I'll find a way to get the money for him. We don't need you," Chastity said infuriated.

"Yeah, whatever," he said.

Chastity got back in the car and headed for Rudy's house.

* * *

When Chastity and Rudy pulled up to her house, she noticed an orange sticker on the door. She parked and got out of the car to see what it said.

Her mouth dropped when she read the words "Eviction notice" on the sticker. She ripped it off and went inside with Rudy along on her heels.

She picked up the mail on the floor, which contained shut-off notices. She sat on the couch with Rudy and read the letters.

"I have 30 days to either pay the rent or be out of her. Where am I gonna get $2,400? I gave that lawyer everything I had trying to help Keem. Then I have 7 days to pay the electric bill, 10 days to pay the water bill, and 10 days to pay the cable bill. What am I gonna do?" she asked, as tears filled her eyes.

Rudy hugged her friend. "It's going to be alright, Chas. I'll see what I can get from my sisters and some of the niggas I fuck with. Why don't you get some money from all those niggas that be sweeting you?"

"Because all they want is some pussy and it belongs to Hakeem," she said confidently.

"You can milk their pockets without giving them any pussy, Chas. I know some girl that works at Set It Off on 2nd and Cambria. I can ask her to get you a job."

"What will I have to do?"

"It's a strip club. All you have to do is dance and collect tips for giving them a private lap dance."

"I can't. That will be cheating on Keem."

"Girl, you need to wise up. That nigga was cheating on you the whole time with that bitch, Meka. You won't be fucking anybody unless you chose to. You'd make so much money because you are prettier than anybody in that bitch. If you want, I'll do it with you," Rudy said, trying to help her friend.

"Give me until tomorrow to think about it. Let's just get some rest for now," Chastity said, as they headed upstairs.

When she reached her room, her cell phone rang. She answered on the third ring. "Hello."

"Hey baby. This is Hakeem."

"Hey, how are you calling this late?" Chastity asked, seeing that it was 11:30 p.m.

"I'm calling from my friend's phone. Look, I only have a couple of minutes so I have to tell you this. I took the deal today for 20 to 40 years. If I had gone to trial, they would have given me 40 years. I heard about how you don't have any money to pay the bills, so go on with your life. If you want the crib, it's yours. I'm going to marry Meka because she is pregnant with my seed, and I don't want the baby to come into the world out of wedlock."

Chastity could not believe what she was hearing. Everything around her became a blur. Rudy was sitting on the bed next to her wondering what he was saying.

"So I'm out here going through all this shit and you call me and say that. You can have that bitch and this fucking house. I hate you, and when I see her, I'm going to whip her ass," Chastity said, as she hung up the phone.

"What happened?" Rudy said, as her friend broke down crying.

Chastity risked everything for him, trying to show how much she loved him, and in turn, he shit on her. She told Rudy everything, as they packed up all her stuff to leave that house once and for all.

She didn't have anywhere to go, so Rudy called Kita and asked if she could stay there for a couple of months until she found a place. Kita gladly agreed.

Chastity reached out to her uncle, but he told her "no" unless she played by his rules. She vowed to get him back one day. She just didn't know when.

* * *

A couple of days later, Rudy and Chastity had an appointment with the manager of Set It Off. They both agreed to become exotic dancers until they saved up enough money to get a place of their own.

The moment he saw Chastity's beautiful body, he knew he had a goldmine and she was hired her on the spot. Rudy was also hired because she was a pretty chocolate goldmine, too. They were scheduled to start that night, which gave them enough time to buy their outfits. Kita had lent them the money because she also knew they would make a lot there. It was money well worth investing.

As they were getting ready in the dressing ready with the other girls, Rudy asked, "Are you nervous?".

"Hell yeah, ain't you?"

"No, because I'm used to attention. What you need is a drink to calm your nerves. I'll go get you something," Rudy said, heading out to the bar.

Rudy had chosen the stage name Moet, because that was her favorite drink. Chastity was given the name White Stallion by the owner, because her ass was so phat, and she looked like she was a white girl.

A couple of minutes later, Rudy came back with two glasses of liquor. "Here you go, girl. It's your favorite drink: Moscato."

"Thank you," she said, grabbing one glass.

Rudy passed her the other one as well. "They're both yours, so drink up because we are about to get paid. I go on stage first and then you will be going. If you get scared, just close your eyes and pretend you're in a room by yourself dancing to the music."

"You're really smart, girl. When I make it, so will you. That is a promise," Chastity said, giving her a hug.

"Okay, let's go show these bitches how two young girls get down," Rudy said, as they went out on the floor.

Chastity had on an all-white thong set with five-inch stilettos. Rudy was wearing a pair of red boy shorts with matching bra and five-inch stilettos. They both let their hair hang down, showing the other girls that they had natural long hair.

Rudy took the stage first as a 2 Chains song came on through the speakers: *"I love bad bitches, that's my fuckin' problem, and yeah, I like to fuck, I gotta fuckin' problem."*

She began dancing to the music, while the crowd threw money at her on the stage. She jumped on the stripper pole, climbing to the top and then sliding down into a split and then bouncing her ass. The crowd was going crazy as Rudy danced to two more songs before her set was over.

Chastity couldn't believe how experienced Rudy was on the pole. They both could dance their asses off, but Rudy looked like she was made for this shit. She went to get another drink before her set when Rudy came down off the stage and walked over to her.

"Girl, you just killed that shit. Where did you learn those moves?" Chastity asked, getting her drink, and gulping it down.

"My sister took us to a striper pole party one time, and we all learned how to hold our balance on it as we slid down. Are you ready to do your thing in a few minutes?"

"Yeah, watching you gave me a couple of ideas for when I get up there."

"Don't worry, you will be just fine. I'm gonna run in the back to freshen up real quick, but I will be back to watch and cheer you on," Rudy said, heading to the dressing room.

Chastity finished off her drink and began feeling real good. Her body was getting real excited. She didn't even notice that Rudy had put a molly in her drink. She was definitely ready for the stage.

"And now making her debut on this stage here tonight, I want all you ballers to get your money out because you're in for a treat. Making her way to the stage, Set It Off presents White Stallion," the DJ announced, as the lights went dark and the florescent beams illuminated the stage. Then all the fog came up from the blowers and the music began to serenade the crowd: *"Temperatures rising, and your body yearning for me. Early and only, I place no one above thee. Oh take me to your ecstasy. . . . "*

Chastity walked towards the pole seductively, spinning around, causing her ass to jump. She started slowly winding down the pole until she reached the floor, going into a split. *"It seems like you're ready (seems like you're ready) to go all the way."* R-Kelly continued to flow through the speakers.

After that song finished, the crowd was focused their attention on to Chastity. Rudy was right there cheering on her friend. The DJ mixed on the board, then Lil Wayne, Juice J, and T.I. came on: *"Bands to make her dance, Bands to make dance, All these bitches poppin' pussy, I'm just poppin' bands. . . ."*

Money began flowing from everywhere around her as White Stallion ripped the stage up. She climbed to the top of the pole, sliding halfway down and then pulling her body out like a flag, making her ass twerk. When she reached the bottom, she laid on the floor, pulled her legs all the way in back of her head, and then poured water into her pussy. Chastity started sliding across the floor until she was near the edge of the stage, and then made her pussy squirt water all over the crowd.

They went into a frenzy, as more and more money hit the stage. By the time she finished her third song, she accumulated over $1,000 on stage. The bouncers had to help her collect all the money off the floor. There were ones, fives, tens, twenties, and even a couple fifties and hundreds laying around her. No one had ever drawn that much attention at one time since Set It Off had opened.

"That's my fuckin' dawg. You tore that bitch up out there. Where the hell did you get those moves? I couldn't believe that was you out there," Rudy said, hugging her friend.

"That came from watching *G String Divas*," Chastity laughed.

She freshened up, changing her outfit, and then they headed out on the floor and entertained the crowd. By the time that they left the club at 2:00 a.m., they were both tired and rich. Rudy drove home so that Chastity could count the money. They had made close to $2,500 just for one night. There was so much more to come, and they couldn't wait.

* * *

Reese and Mal were at the trap house counting and wrapping up the new work they just copped from their new connect.

"This shit ain't gonna sell, man. We shouldn't have ever got this shit from that nigga. The potency of this shit wouldn't even get my dog high," Mal said frustrated.

"Just chill, nigga! This is all we got right now until we find an out-of-town connect."

"Why can't we just deal with the nigga Keem was fucking with? All we need is his cell phone from that bitch."

"He's not gonna deal with us. We took all of Keem's money and the rest of the work out of his crib. Then on top of that, we didn't even pay for his lawyer. He was supposed to be our friend, and we basically said fuck you to him. So you can damn sure bet that he let that nigga know not to mess with us," Reese said, taking the gloves off after he put all the work in the bags.

93

"How about we just tell Keem that his girl did get the money, but she kept it all to herself. He will believe us over her anyway."

"Let's go see him and find out."

* * *

When Hakeem came out from the back and saw Mal and Reese sitting there, he gave them a look of disappointment. Instead of turning around though, he wanted to see what they had to say.

They stood up when he approached them. "What's up Hakeem? How have you been holding up?" Reese asked.

"Why are you niggas here? You stole all my cash from me and now you have the audacity to come up here and see me like everything is good."

"Hold up, man. That's why we are here. We didn't take your money. We gave it to Chastity when she came for it. Why would we take money that we all worked hard to get? That bitch has been lying to you, man. Trying to put the blame on us," Mal said.

Keem sat there thinking for a while about who was telling the truth. Was it his boys who he grew up with and had never done him dirty before or was it his girl that found out about his baby momma, came from nothing, and now she had become well liked. What would make people act like this? Money! He decided to see what they were really there for.

"So what made y'all come see me besides this?"

"We wanted you to talk to your connect and plug us in, because we have bullshit compared to what we had when you were home," Reese said

He knew then that they really did take the money and keep it. He just needed to prove it. What they didn't know was that he had somebody watching Chastity's spending habits to see if she really had the money. So far, she was out there struggling.

"I'll send him word to contact y'all. I'm not sure if he'll deal or not, but I'll try," Keem said, getting up and leaving without even saying bye to Reese or Mal.

If you bitch-ass niggas are lying, I'll find out. And when this reduction of sentencing goes through, it's y'all ass, he thought to himself, as he walked through the visiting room door.

THIRTEEN

FOR THE LAST MONTH, Chastity and Rudy worked at Set It Off on Fridays and Saturdays. They were making really good money there, so they decided to work during the week as well. Neither of them went to school any longer because they were typically making more money doing private parties for businessmen.

Chastity wouldn't have sex with anybody because she didn't want to go out like that. Rudy, on the other hand, was fucking like a champ in the private rooms. She was really all about a dollar.

One Friday night, the club was packed with people spending money. Chastity had just finished her set and she was now in the back changing when one of the other dancers came in.

"White Stallion, you have a special request in the VIP room. They only want a dance from you?"

"Who are they?"

"Two fine-ass niggas, but it's only one that is requesting a dance from you," the dancer said and then walked back out.

Chastity got ready and then headed to the VIP room. When she walked in, her heart stopped. It was her Uncle Tony sitting on the couch, rubbing himself.

"Hey Chastity... I mean White Stallion. So this is what you been up to, huh? I always knew you had what it takes," he said, looking at her body while licking his lip.

"What do you want, Uncle Tony?"

"I just came to get a lap dance from my favorite niece. Now get over here and give me what I'm paying for."

"No, find someone else to get a dance from. You are my uncle, not some dude from the street," Chastity said, walking away.

"Does the owner know your real age?"

That comment made her stop and turn around. She looked at Tony momentarily and then said, "Why are you doing this? I'm out here on my own trying to make it. You kicked me out as if I was nothing. Now you're trying to get me fired from my job."

"All I want is one dance and I'll leave," he said.

Chastity didn't want to lose her job, but she was also tired of her uncle's abusive ways.

"No, I'm not doing it. Do what you have to do, but if you do say anything to them, you will regret it. I promise you that."

"Are you threatening me, little girl?" he said, standing up. He walked over to her and was readying to smack her when a bouncer walked in.

"I think it's time for you to get the fuck out of here before they have to carry you out."

Tony saw the look in his eyes and knew it was time to roll out. He He left the club without saying anything.

"Thank you," she said, as he walked out the door.

Feeling relieved, Chastity sighed and went back on the floor to make some more money.

* * *

The night was over and Chastity and Rudy were on their way out the door, when one of the bouncers told them that the manager wanted to see them. They stopped in his office and sat in the chairs next to the desk.

"I'm gonna ask you a question, and I only want the truth so we won't have to go any further, okay?" he said to them.

They both nodded their heads, as they wondered what the conversation was about.

"How old are you girls?"

Chastity knew exactly what was going on now. She wanted to lie, but it would come back and hurt her late.

"We're 16, but we both will be 17 next month," she said, hoping that would work.

"Are you fucking kidding me? Do you know how much trouble I could get into if this place was raided? Both of you leave now and don't come back here until you're at least 18. This guy threatened to have my place shut down if he sees y'all in here again."

"Is there anything we can do to change your mind? How will we be able to take care of ourselves?" Rudy asked.

"No, there isn't! I can't have this type of drama in my life. Leave now, and you can keep everything you made tonight," he said, picking up his ringing phone.

Chastity and Rudy stormed out of the club angry. No words were spoken between them until they were on the 95 heading home.

"This nigga done made us get fired, because I won't let him touch me. I feel like killing him," Chastity said.

"Who are you talking about?"

Chastity finally broke down and told Rudy the whole story about her uncle's perverted, ancestral ways. She even told her how he came in the club that night trying to do it again. Rudy was even more pissed off than she was.

"One day, we are going to teach him a lesson. Don't worry girl, we are friends, and I'll never let him hurt you again," Rudy said.

Chastity didn't realize that she was speeding until she heard the highway patrol siren behind her.

"Holy shit!" she said, pulling over.

The cop waited until two more cars pulled up before getting out of his car and approaching the vehicle. Chastity rolled down the window and waited.

"I pulled you over for doing 82 in a 55 zone. Can you please step out of the vehicle? Both of you," he instructed.

They both stepped out of the car, waiting for further instructions.

"Whose car is this you're driving?" one officer asked.

"My boyfriend's, but he is locked up," Chastity answered.

"Well, I hate to tell you this, but this is a stolen car. I'm going to have to place you both under arrest for receiving stolen property," the officer said, as the female officer who just pulled up began to search them. Once she frisked them, they were placed in separate police cars and taken back to the precinct for processing.

Chastity was scared because she had never been arrested before. She never even rode in the back of a police car. It seemed as if everything was starting to fall apart for her now. She remembered what her grandma used to say, "When it rains, it pours, so remember all good things come to an end."

These words had true meaning. All she was trying to do was make enough money to afford her own place, but her uncle, and now Keem, had ruined that for her temporarily. She thought about what she was going to do before, and then she decided when she got out of this, she would make the call.

* * *

Three hours later, Chastity and Rudy were released from custody into Kita's care. Since they were both minors, they essentially received a slap on the wrist. However, it was due to the fact that the girls didn't know the car was stolen.

When they got home, Chastity showered and made something to eat. She, Rudy, and Kita were sitting in the kitchen talking. She told Kita about Keem, but not her uncle. That was she and Rudy's secret.

"I can't believe his nut ass didn't tell you that you were picking up a stolen car. This shit is crazy, but at least y'all are home. I'll see y'all later, I have something to take care of," Kita said, leaving out the door.

"I'll be right back, I have to make a phone call," Chastity said, as she grabbed her purse and went upstairs.

When she went into Rudy's room, she locked the door behind her and sat on the bed. She pulled out Hakeem's cell phone and looked through the address book. Once she found the number she was looking for, she hit the call button.

"Hello," someone answered after three rings.

Chastity didn't respond at first. She wanted to hang up because she didn't know what to say.

"Hello," he said, one more time.

"Um, hello, is this Chris?"

"Yeah, who is this calling me on Keem's phone?"

"This is Chastity, the girl that went to Miami with him. I was just calling to see if you need me to go out . . . ."

"Whoa, ma, not on the phone. Where are you at right now, so that we can talk face to face?" Chris said, cutting her off.

"I'm home."

"Where is home?"

"I'm in Wilson projects with my best friend," Chastity said.

"Well, meet me at the park where they play basketball on 25th and Snyder in about 15 minutes, and then we'll talk then."

"Okay, I'll see you when I get there," she said before hanging up.

She hoped what she was attempting to do wouldn't get her into any trouble or hurt. She searched through her bag and put on a pair of all-black tights and a tank top with the word "rebel" written across it. She told Rudy that she was on her way to the store.

"Bring two dutches back with you, bitch. I'm going to take a shower because I still smell the funk from that holding cell on me," Rudy said, heading upstairs.

By the time that Chastity got to the basketball court, an apple red Lexus was waiting. It had dark tint, so she wasn't sure who was actually see inside. She didn't know that it was Chris until he rolled down the window.

"Chastity, get in," he said.

She walked over and hopped into the car. The seat was nice and comfortable, and the AC was cold. It felt so good in the car and the air made her nipples hard.

"So what can I do for you, baby girl? And please don't be wasting my time," he said firmly.

"I know you don't really know me, but Hakeem did me wrong, and his friends took all his money and left us broke. I'm trying to make some money so that I can take care of myself. If you pay me, I am willing to go back out to Miami for you."

"No disrespect to you, ma, but before we go any further, lift your shirt up a little. It's for my own protection," Chris said, as he watched her lift up her shirt.

"Did you think I was trying to set you up? I wouldn't do anything like that," she said, fixing her shirt.

"Just making sure, that's all. Now, I do have an open spot, but you can't go by yourself. Do you have someone that you trust with your life?"

"Yes, my best friend Rudy. She is more like a sister to me. She and her sisters are letting me stay with them until I can get my own place."

"Well, I'll tell you what I'll do. If you make a couple of runs for me, I will get my friend to rent you one of her apartments. Plus, you will get paid for your trips out there. You don't have to worry about paying for anything when you get there, because everything is on the house," Chris said, getting her attention.

"You would do that for me?"

"Consider it as an investment for future employment. I take care of those who take care of me. So do we have a deal, yes or no?"

"Yes, we have a deal. I'll let my friend know what's going on when I get home."

"Okay, get packed up, because y'all will be heading to the airport in the morning. I'll pick both of you up around 10:00, so be ready."

Chastity got out of the car and ran back home to tell her friend the good news. She just hoped that she was with it.

FOURTEEN

THE NEXT DAY, CHASTITY and Rudy arrived in Miami, and just as last time, the driver was waiting at the arrival gate. This time though, he was holding up a sign that read "Chastity." The girls walked over and jumped into the limo.

"Damn, I feel like a fucking celebrity riding in style like this," Rudy said, as she relaxed in the comfortable seats.

"Remember why we are here though, okay? I don't want them to look at us as just two young girls trying to make some money."

"We *are* two young girls trying to make some money," Rudy said smiling.

Chastity couldn't reply, so she simply laughed at her friend. The driver pulled up to the Hilton Hotel and let the girls out. He gave them their room key while passing their luggage to the bellhop who escorted them to their room

"I will be on call if you need me for anything. The club will open at 9:00. What time would you like me to pick you up?" the driver asked.

"10:00 will be good," Chastity said, as, they followed the bellhop into their room.

After settling into the spacious suite, they changed into their swimsuits.

"Let's go turn some heads on this beach," Rudy said, in her lime-green bikini set. It was so small that when she bent over, it looked as if she was wearing a thong.

Chastity was no better. She wore a white bikini with red stripes that made her ass look tight and firm. They both rocked Chanel sunglasses.

"Let's go! Don't forget your phone just in case your lil' jump-off calls you," Chastity said smiling.

"At least I have a jump-off to jump on this when I need it," she said, grabbing her ass. "You're gonna grow cobwebs in your shit if you don't get you some dick soon."

"Is that all that's on your mind? I'm trying to get paid, not laid, so let's go enjoy this weather for a while. We'll go get a massage afterwards... my treat."

"Sounds good to me," Rudy said, as they headed out of the hotel room.

When they made it to the beach, it was in full swing. They rented beach chairs and then laid them out on the sand. Chastity put sun tan lotion on her body before sitting on the chair to enjoy the sun's rays. Rudy put up an umbrella to prevent getting any blacker than she already was.

While they were chilling, a guy wearing a pair of Speedos came up to them. Rudy stared at his dick instead of his face.

"Can I offer you ladies a drink?" he asked.

"No thank you," Chastity said.

"We'll take two strawberry daiquiris, please. My friend is a little shy with strangers," Rudy said, giving Chastity a wink.

"I'll be right back then," he said while walking off.

"Here you go with your fake-ass making shit up again. I can't take you anywhere without you wanting to flirt with people," Chastity told Rudy, as she pulled her shades up.

"Don't hate the playa, hate the game," she said, as they both shared a laugh waiting for the man in tights to come back with their drinks.

* * *

After the beach, they returned to the hotel and enjoyed a delightful massage that involved a seaweed bath, waxing, facials, hot stones, and more. By the time they made it back to the hotel room, they felt extra good. Since they only had a couple of hours to get ready for the club, they decided to pick out what they were going to wear and begin getting ready.

An hour and a half later, Chastity and Rudy looked into the mirror, gazing at how stunning they looked.

Chastity was rocking a white, two-piece, crystal-embellished collar top, with a skirt to match. She had on a pair of Christian Louboutin's on her feet and a purse to set off the outfit.

Rudy also looked stellar, wearing a red, strapless Alexander McQueen mini dress with a pair of Alexander McQueen shoes. The dresses were fitting the both of them like gloves.

They made their way down to the lobby to wait for the driver. All eyes were on them as if they were stars. An all-black Aston Martin pulled up in the parking lot, dropping the mouths of everyone standing there, including Chastity and Rudy's.

The girls didn't know that the car was there for them until the driver got out and opened the door.

"Whenever you're ready, ladies," the driver said, patiently waiting for them to hop in.

They got in the car and the driver took them to Club Bamboo.

* * *

"Call the investor's tomorrow morning and let them know that we're interested in buying the property on McDade Boulevard. Tell them to get with our attorneys and draw up a contract so we can sign off on it," Pedro toldo his secretary.

He and E.J. sat in the office of the club discussing business on a conference call with his secretary. They would do business any time of the day, so it wasn't strange to be handling shit at 10:20 at night. After ending the call, Pedro braked from his work to fix himself a drink.

"So have you done the finalization on that project in Atlanta yet?" E.J. asked.

"Everything should be signed and paid for by Friday. Whenever you want to visit, we can," Pedro said, taking a sip of his drink.

"Good to hear. Did the two girls get here yet that Chris sent?"

"Nobody came to notify me yet, but they should be here anytime now. Why are you even worried about that anyway? You're retired, so keep it that way. That part of the business is all on me, okay partner?" Pedro said smirking.

"Okay, okay. I was just asking a question; and you're right, I shouldn't be worrying about the drug game anymore. You and Chris are doing a marvelous job. I'll guess I'll be heading down on the floor to find me a Spanish mommy to take home," E.J. said, getting up and heading for the door.

"What time are you leaving?" Pedro asked.

"Maybe closing time. I'm just gonna chill for a while."

"Oh, alright."

E.J. started towards the bar, when he noticed two fine-ass ladies being escorted to the VIP area.

One in particular caught his attention. She looked to be a combination of Spanish and Caucasian, and rocked a tight-ass white dress. As they passed him, he noticed that she looked familiar. He didn't know from where, but he made a mental note to find out.

"Damn, you know that sexy nigga right there sporting that Versace suit? Cause he damn sure thinks he knows you, the way he's staring," Rudy said.

"Girl, shut up! How am I going to know him when I don't even live out here?"

"You don't have to live out here to know people, Chas. Look over there. Isn't that Khloe Kardashian and French Montana right there? Oh shit, and look at Kelly Rowland and

Gabriele Union sitting over there. I'm in love with this club, girl. We definitely have to come back out here," Rudy said excited.

Before they reached their table, E.J. stopped them. "Excuse me, but do I know you?"

"Why does everybody use that same lame-ass line? No, you don't know me because we never met, and I'm not interested," Chastity said, clearly irritated. They continued walking and sat down in the VIP section.

"That was rude, Chas. Why would you talk to him like that? He only asked you a question."

Chastity didn't even respond. Instead, she began moving in her seat to the music. She noticed him staring at her for a minute and then began talking to the bartender.

Twenty minutes later, the waitress came over and told Chastity and Rudy to follow her up to the office. They entered the office and they were greeted by Pedro.

"Well, hello again, Chastity. Thank you for deciding to become a part of the team. This must be the lovely Rudy. You are surely a beautiful young lady," he said, kissing the back of her hand.

"Thank you," Rudy said as she blushed.

"Well, have you ladies enjoyed your stay so far?"

"This place is the bomb. You have so many celebrities here tonight. Is it always like this?" Rudy asked.

"Well, I can't take the credit for that. The owner is a very poplar man," he said, looking at the screen. "As a matter of fact, here he comes now."

Chastity looked at the monitor and couldn't believe who was about to come into the office. "Oh shit, that's who it is," she said to herself.

Rudy looked to see who was coming in the door. She smiled at Chastity and said, "You turned a rich man down. You go, girl."

For the next few minutes, Pedro explained to the girls what they would be doing and what time to meet him the next day. After the meeting, the girls left and E.J. came out from behind them.

"Chastity, hold up a minute," he said, walking up to them. The music was too loud so he pulled her outside.

"I didn't mean any disrespect earlier so don't take it like that. I'm just interested in getting to know you. I know you're leaving to go back to Philly tomorrow, but can we have breakfast before you go?" he asked her.

"I don't mean to be rude either, but I'm tired of dealing with rich guys, because all they want to do is spoil me with gifts. I want to be able to make my own way, so I'm going to decline on your offer," Chastity said.

"I feel you, but if you ever want to talk, give me a call," he said, as he passed her his number and walked away.

"Damn, that's the second time tonight that you turned that fine-ass nigga down. If you don't want him, give him to me, and I'll show you what to do with him," Rudy said smiling

Chastity couldn't help but smile at her freaky-ass friend. They went to enjoy the rest of the night.

* * *

The next morning, Chastity woke up and looked at her cell phone. She had five missed calls. They were all from Chris. Chastity realized that she overslept and was late for their pick up. She immediately called Chris back.

"Yo, where the hell are you at? You are 45 minutes late for your pick up. Pedro's men are outside your hotel room. Open the door, handle that, and hurry because your plane leaves in one hour," Chris said, hanging up the phone in her ear.

Chastity woke up Rudy before throwing on a robe and opening the door.

Two giants stood on the other side of the door waiting. They walked into the suite without saying a word. They searched every room of the suite, making sure they were alone before anybody spoke.

"Take off your robes," one of the men said to the girls.

Rudy looked like she was about to curse them out until she saw Chastity letting her robe fall to the floor. She nodded at Rudy, and she did the same thing. They were both standing there with panties and bras on.

The men opened the briefcase and pulled out the keys and tape. First, they taped six keys to Rudy, and then they started doing the same thing to Chastity. One of the men purposely rubbed Chastity's ass while he placed the tape around her body. When she looked at him, he continued to smile at her.

Once they were done, they walked toward the door. "You have to get to the airport in 45 minutes if you don't want to miss your flight. Leave everything except for what you're wearing out of here. You will be reimbursed when you're back safely. The driver is waiting downstairs, so don't be wasting any more time," he said as they left.

Chastity and Rudy rushed to throw on clothes and ran out the door, trying not to miss their flight.

When they got to the airport, they made it just in time. Chastity knew she was going to hear it when they got home. She was just hoping that he would still do business with her. If he did, she said that she would never make that mistake again.

"So what are we going to do for our birthday next week?" Rudy asked, as the plane took off.

"I don't know, but I'm partying that whole day and night. We have to enjoy ourselves for sure."

"Yeah, that's what we'll do. How much are they gonna pay us for this?"

"We never talked about it, but I'm sure it will be something nice and sweet. They do great business from what Keem used to tell me."

"Okay, we'll let the money begin flowing 'cause we are getting that apartment real soon," Rudy said, putting on her earphones and pressing play on her IPod.

Chastity blankly stared out the window thinking about the risk that she and her friend were taking. She was trying to figure out what else she could do to get this money. She thought about Keem's phone again and an idea came to mind. She just had to wait until they returned home to see if it world work.

FIFTEEN

"YOU ALMOST BLEW A major deal today. That kind of mistake can never happen again," Chris said to Chastity as they sat in his car.

She and Rudy had made it back safely. Now they were waiting to see how much they were going to get paid. He passed an envelope to Chastity while he placed the keys in the stash spot of the car.

"That's 10 grand in there. Both of y'all get five a piece. Can you make another trip in two weeks?"

"Yeah, we sure can, and don't worry. I won't make that mistake again. I know time is money," Chastity said, as she and Rudy got out of the car.

"Yo, I almost forgot to give you this," Chris said, passing her another envelope. "It's another $5,000 for the stuff you had to leave in Miami. That should cover everything."

"Thank you, Chris. See you later."

They went into the house and split up the money between them. They both had $7,500 apiece. Chastity called the realtor that Chris told her about and set up an appointment so she could see the apartments. After she hung up, she laid on the couch and napped.

Rudy hung up her phone from talking to some dude she knew. She looked at Chastity on the couch.

"I'll be back, I'm about to go over Budda's house for a few minutes. Do you want to come?"

"No, I'm good, but when you come back, I want to talk to you about something. I'll have all the answers by the time you get back."

"Okay," Rudy said, heading out the door.

Instead of resting, Chastity decided to make the calls that would hopefully change her life. She dialed the first number from Keem's phone, and the person answered on the second ring.

"Damn, nigga, you finally made it home. It's been real fucked up around here lately."

"This is not Hakeem, my name is Chastity."

"Who the fuck is you, and why do you have my boy's phone?" the man said.

"I was his girl until he got locked up. I'm taking over his business and I wanted to know if you would be interested in going though me? I have access to the same connect that he was dealing with. Do you want to get the work from me?" Chastity asked.

The dude wanted to cop the shit he was getting from Keem, because what he had now was garbage. He decided to text her and then see if she knew what she was doing. He used to get fifty bundles from him for $1,400.

"So you're gonna sell me the 50 bundles for $1,000 a pop, just like he did?"

"Yes, and you will only deal with me, right?"

The man smiled, because he knew that he was about to get over on her. "You got a deal, ma. When can I get the first pack, because I have a client that's ready to bail on me if I don't get that good shit?" he said.

"I will call you back within a couple of hours and let you know what time we can meet."

"Don't forget to hit me up. I'll be waiting," he said, before they hung up.

Chastity smiled, but she didn't know what she was getting into. She called the three other people in his phone and told them the same thing. Since she got a price from the first dude she talked to, she threw that number out there to them as well. They thought it was a joke, but agreed to do business with her. She was about to lose money and didn't even know it. Now that part one was done, it was time for the next phase of the plan. She had to get Chris to let her get some work.

Chastity didn't know how to negotiate deals, so she decided to get some lessons from somebody that did. Kita's boyfriend was doing big shit in the streets, so she was going to get her to ask him to teach her the ropes. She would do that when she got back from her appointment.

* * *

"Where have you been for the last couple of days? I've been trying to hook up with you, but you never responded to my calls or text," Budda said.

"It don't matter where I was. I'm here now, so what's up?"

"You already know what's up. Come over here," he said, grabbing Rudy and pulling her onto his lap.

She straddled his body as he gripped her ass. She had on a skirt, so he instantly had access to her heated pussy.

"Ummm, stick it in. I've been horny for two days now, and you better not cum fast or this will be your last time hitting this," she said, grinding on his dick.

Budda unzipped his shorts and pulled his dick out. He grabbed one of the condoms off the table, put it on, and prepared himself for Rudy's wet pussy. He moved her panties to the side and slid right in.

"Oh shit, you feel so good," he said, as Rudy moved up and down on his dick.

He squeezed her ass cheeks together, while she tightened her pussy muscles, making it hard for him to hold back. Whatever Rudy did, he could never last longer than five minutes. He felt his nut rising, so he pulled out of her.

"Turn around and sit on this dick so I can enjoy it a little longer," he told her.

Rudy already knew he was trying to stop himself from busting too soon because she felt him tensing up. She took off her panties, sat back on his dick, bouncing faster, and harder while trying to get hers before he got his. It never happened, even with a condom on, he still shot his load before her.

Frustrated, she got up and sat on the couch, opening her legs. "Come eat my pussy until I come."

"Now you're mad at me, huh? I don't feel like doing that today. I have some shit that I have to do, so hit me up later," he said, fixing his clothes.

"Nigga, you know what?" she said, standing up, "This was your last time touching me. Don't fucking call me anymore. As a matter of fact, lose my number with your broke ass."

"That's cool. I got bitches on deck just for times like this," he said, throwing her a $20 bill.

"I don't need your money, pussy. I got my own."

"Now you don't need my money, huh? Okay, when you do need it, let me know and I might just let you get some."

Rudy stormed out the door mad and still horny. She was tired of his whack-ass anyway. She headed back home to see if Chastity was ready to talk yet.

* * *

Mal and Reese were driving down Lancaster Avenue looking for a place to park so that they could grab something to eat from Let's Grub. They hadn't made any money lately because the dope they were selling was garbage, just like everybody else's they knew. There was only two niggas in Philly that had really good dope, but they wouldn't tell anybody who their connect was. They were making all the money in the city.

"Yo, ain't that Pooch right there in that Chrysler 300?" Reese said, looking at the dude talking on the phone.

"Yeah, pull up on the side of him. I hope he has that money he owes me or else his ass is done!"

They pulled right beside him and Mal jumped out of the car. They had him boxed in so he couldn't go anywhere. When he saw who it was, he damn near shit on himself. He didn't know what to do.

"What's up, Pooch? You got that cash for me or what? I've been waiting for three weeks, and I'm not waiting any longer," Mal said.

Reese jumped out of the car and stood next to Mal, waiting for him to make a move.

"Mal, shit's been slow man, but I will have your money for you soon. I was out of town the last couple of days and nothing was jumping."

Mal, tired of his lies, opened the car door and pulled Pooch out. Reese and Mal began stomping Pooch in front of his car and didn't care who was watching.

"I'm 'a give till Friday to get my fucking money, you clown-ass nigga. If I have to come looking for you, I'm 'a pop you," Mal said.

Reese went in his pockets and took the money that he had. They hopped in the car and sped off.

"That nigga just ruined my dad. I'm tired of being broke, so let's go grab our straps. It's hunting season, and if niggas ain't trying to get down, then they're gonna lay down," Reese said.

"I'm with you, my nigga. It's time to get paid."

Chastity and Rudy had just met Tiffany and they gave her the deposit for a two-bedroom apartment in the University City area of west Philly. They gave her $1,950, plus an extra $3,900 for the first six months. She gave them the keys on the spot thanks to Chris for keeping his word and calling Tiff to set it up.

Tiffany didn't stay in Philly anymore. She had a nice and very large crib out in Meredith Township. She owned all the apartment complexes on 40th Baring and 40th Brown. She let Chastity move into the one on Baring Street.

"Let's go hit the store up and get some furniture for our place," Chastity said, as they rode in the car with Sharon.

"Where are we going to grab something from?" Rudy asked.

"I'll take y'all over to Seaman's Furniture store. They can deliver everything today, so y'all will be able to move right in tonight. They will even set everything up," Sharon said.

"Well, our birthdays are Friday and Saturday, so we have to have a party somewhere," Chastity said.

Chastity and Rudy's birthdays were only a day apart. People said that's why the two were so close. Others thought they were messing around because they were always together. They were so close because they could relate to one another.

"How about we have our party at Club Ziaire's?"

"Call them and set it up. Let them know that we'll bring the money pass tonight after we get settled in. You're gonna take us, right Sharon?" Chastity asked.

"Yeah, of course, I will. How else will y'all be getting there? We need to rent a car for this weekend though, because Sean is going to need his car. They are going to Howard University to his frat party."

"You don't ever think he's cheating on you when he goes to those sorority parties?" Chastity asked her.

"For what? That shit don't stress me out, because I don't let it. Besides, everybody cheats; you just have to know how and when. The biggest rule of cheating is just don't get caught," Sharon said, as they pulled into Seaman's parking lot.

They went in and spent $5,000 on furniture for their apartment. When they do their next trip, they were going to get some more stuff. They didn't want to spend too much money because of the party.

After they paid for everything, they went shopping for the clothes they were going to wear on Friday. Chastity looked for something exclusive that no one had ever seen yet. She was trying to turn every niggas head in the club as soon as they saw her.

Rudy already knew what she was going to wear. She had seen it while they were in Miami riding along their "Rodeo Drive." She was hoping that she could find it here, because if not, she would have to order it and have it sent overnight delivery.

SIXTEEN

CLUB ZIAIRE WAS JAMMED packed when Chastity, Rudy, Kita, and Sharon pulled up in a rented Navigator limo. Inside of the club was equipped with a bar, television, and a host of other necessities. They wanted to pull up in style, which was exactly what they did. All eyes were on them as they stepped out of the limo. Kita and Sharon both had on Chanel pencil dresses. Sharon's wore a red dress and Kita's was gold.

Rudy was dressed in a black Jason Wu strapless dress that fell just above her knees. She wore a pair of black Jason Wu five-inch stilettos to match. Her goal was to steal the show, at least until Chastity stepped out of the limo.

Chastity had on a white Vera Wang dress that left nothing to the imagination. It also fell to just above her knees, but had a slit that came halfway up the side. It fit her to a tee, hugging her body in all the right places, and left her back exposed. She wore on five-inch stilettos with straps that went up to her mid-calf.

Both girls captured everyone in the room's attention as they walked into the club. Making their way to the VIP section where their birthday cake waited for them, the girls ignored the crowd of men trying to holler at them. They spoke and kept it moving. When they finally made it to their booth, Neatra had it all set up for the birthday girls. She arrived earlier in the day so that she could get everything ready.

"'Bout time you bitches made it here," she said, giving hugs to all her sisters and Chastity.

"You know we had to make a grand entrance. That way all those bitches out there can be jealous of us," Kita said, pointing to the crowd.

There were so many bottles of liquor on the table, courtesy of Chris, that they couldn't choose what they wanted to try first.

"Hey ladies, I hope that you enjoy yourselves tonight. Drinks are on the house," Chris said standing there.

"Is this your club or something?" Chastity asked.

"No, this is my wife and brother's club. He named it after his son who died when he was three. Now my wife runs it by herself, with a little help from me."

"Well thank you for the hospitality that you're showing us. We are going to have a ball here tonight," Chastity said.

"Don't mention it. If you need me, I'll be up in the office with my wife finishing up some paperwork."

"I have to ask you something before you leave. Can we talk in private? It will only take a minute," Chastity said

She followed him over to a small office where only security were allowed in. He closed the door behind him so that the loud music was now at a muted level.

"What's on your mind?" he asked Chastity.

"Well, I was trying to do something other than carrying drugs back from Miami. I called all of Hakeem's people the other day, and they said that they were willing to deal with me."

"So, do you really think that you can handle something like that? This is a drastic step up that you are trying to take. Do you even know how much to sell or buy the work for?" he asked.

"Well, they asked me if I would still give it to them for the same price that Hakeem gave to them. I told them yeah. He charged the guys $1,000 for every 50 bundles."

"Wait a minute! Who told you some bullshit like that?"

"This guy named Tee. Why?"

"Listen, this guy was about to get over on you. Keem never sold him no 50 bundles for $1,000. Everything is $1,400 or more. Did anybody else tell you that?" he asked.

"No, but when I called them, I kind of told them the same thing," Chastity said, looking kind of crazy.

"You know what, if you really want to do something other than taking that trip, I have something for you."

"What will I have to do?"

"You'll be my pick-up and drop-off person until you learn the game. You will drop the work off to people and pick up the money. If anybody gives you any trouble, let me know and they will be dealt with. I want you to meet me tomorrow and we'll go over everything that you will be doing. Nobody will be dealing with me from now on; it will be you. Go ahead and enjoy your party. Tell Rudy I said happy birthday."

"Thank you, Chris. And I'll be ready tomorrow when you pick me up," Chastity said, heading for the door.

"By the time I finish molding you, you will be running your own empire. You will still have to make that last run for me, so you and Rudy need to be ready to leave."

They both left the office and returned to the party. The music was jumping and the crowd was wild. Chastity went on the floor with her friends and they all started dancing.

* * *

It was 2:00 a.m. and the party was over. Chastity was both tipsy and horny. She hadn't had sex since her man, who was now her ex, was arrested. She used her sex toys often, but tonight she needed the real thing. Sharon and Kita had left a half hour earlier. Neatra was about to leave with some dude she was messing with, while Rudy was drunk and waiting for the limo to pull up.

Chastity danced with some dude all night, and she wanted to give him a chance to show his moves in a bed. She wouldn't usually do this, but tonight she was feeling frisky.

"Can you help me take my friend to the limo?' she said to the dude she danced with.

"Where is y'all parked at?" he asked, helping Rudy walk outside.

"Right in front of the door. Do you have some place to be right now or are you are free?'

"Why, what's up?"

"I could use some company tonight, and since you are cute, I would like for you to come back to my crib," Chastity said boldly.

"Let me just let my boys know to roll out without me and I'll be right back," he said, running back into the club.

A couple of minutes later he came back out and jumped in the limo. They headed back to Chastity and Rudy's apartment. The dude sat next to Chastity, but the whole time he was looking under Rudy's dress, because she had her legs wide open, as she lay back asleep.

He put his hand on Chastity's leg, rubbing her knee. She grabbed his hand looking at him. He thought she was going to push him away, but to his delight, she put his hand between her legs and let him feel how wet she was.

"Damn, I hope you can handle all of this," she said, opening and shutting her legs to his touch.

"Let's find out," he said, getting on his knees.

He slid her panties to the side and began eating her pussy right in the Navigator. She leaned her head back and grabbed his head as he devoured her pussy.

"That's right, nigga, eat this pussy. Oh shit, yes, right there. That is my fucking spot!" she said, while on the verge of releasing her juices all over his face.

He drank every ounce of her cum, making her want to fuck him in the limo. He pulled out his dick and was readying to enter her drenched pussy, when she stopped him.

"Wait, we're almost at my apartment."

"Let me just get a taste of what's to come. I just want to stick the head in, that's all."

"Nope, I don't fuck strangers without a condom. We will be there in five minutes, so just hold up."

"Damn, I'm gonna have blue balls by the time we get to your crib," he said, fixing his pants.

"Don't worry, it will be worth the wait," she said smiling.

They arrived at the apartment, and the dude carried Rudy into the crib, while Chastity opened the door for them.

"Take her to that room on the left. You can go into the other room and wait while I take a quick shower," she said, as she went into the bathroom.

The dude helped Rudy into her room and laid her on the bed. He was about to leave the room, when temptation got the best of him. He looked at her lying there, and then went over and slid her panties to the side. She squirmed when he put a finger in her love tunnel. He started fingering her pussy until she started moving to the rhythm of this hand.

"Mmmmm," she said, opening her legs wider.

He pulled out his dick and put it on her wet lips as he kept finger fucking her. He was about to fuck her when he heard the shower turn off. He quickly ran out of Rudy's room and into Chastity's.

Chastity walked into the room butt naked with her clothes in her hand. "Are you ready for this?" she asked, bouncing her ass.

He took off his clothes and lay in the bed. Chastity climbed on the bed and reached on her nightstand in her purse. She pulled out a condom and gave it to him. She picked up the remote to the surround sound and pressed play on the entertainment system. *Dance for You* by Beyoncé filled the room, as she stood over top of him dancing seductively to the music.

He quickly pulled the condom on over his dick anticipating what she was about to do. The moment it was on, Chastity slid down on his dick.

"That's right, girl, ride this dick!" he said, as he pumped in and out of her tight hole.

Chastity needed this so bad that she began bouncing faster and faster on his dick. She came two minutes later.

She rolled over and put her ass in the air so he could hit it from the back. The dude quickly complied by sliding right in. They fucked long and hard for the next hour, before Chastity fell asleep exhausted.

* * *

The next morning Chastity woke up with a headache. She couldn't even remember what happened that night besides fucking some dude that she didn't even get a chance to ask his name. She looked at her phone to see what time it was. It was only 10:00 a.m., so she went into the kitchen to make herself some breakfast.

A few minutes later, Rudy walked into the kitchen still wearing her dress from the night before.

"Good morning, Ms. Drunk," Chastity said.

"Hey bitch, make me some of whatever you're making. I had a crazy ass dream last night."

"Oh boy, what happened to your freak-ass this time?" Chastity said, setting the plates of bacon and cheese eggs on the table for Rudy and herself.

"I had a dream last night that I was sucking somebody's dick, and they were playing with my pussy. Girl, that shit felt like the real thing, 'cause when I woke up this morning my panties had dry cum stains in them. Damn... just thinking about that shit has a bitch all hot and bothered."

"Well no one came in here with you last night except me and this nigga I met at the club."

"So you finally cleaned out the cobwebs on that coochie of yours. Did he tear that shit up, because you look brand new," Rudy asked, while eating a piece of toast.

"I don't remember too much about last night; and if he would have blown my back out, then my shit would be sore right now"

"He must have had a little dick then," Rudy said, holding up her thumb and index finger. They both laughed while they finished eating their food.

"I have to get dressed because I have some business to discuss with Chris today. If everything goes right, we are about to get paid," Chastity said, rinsing the dishes before putting them in the dishwasher.

"Before you go, do you even remember the dude's name that you were laid up with? Where did he go?" Rudy asked.

"No, I didn't get his name, because he was a one-night stand that I definitely won't be seeing anymore hopefully."

Rudy followed her to her room as Chastity made sure she still had her money from last night. It was all still in her purse.

"I don't even know how the nigga got home this morning or what time he left. I hope I didn't give his little dick self my number."

"I guess I taught you well, bitch. See you later. I'm going to lay back down for a while until you return from your meeting. Then I'm gonna treat you to lunch for our birthday," Rudy said, leaving Chastity to get dressed for her meeting with Chris.

SEVENTEEN

CHRIS PICKED UP CHASTITY around 11:30 a.m. and took her out to his stash spot. It wasn't too far from where she lived. They pulled up to the spot on 52nd and Reno and parked.

"Come on in," Chris said, getting out of the car.

Chastity followed him into his crib and sat down at the kitchen table. Chris showed her how to access the floor safe that contained the dope that she would be distributing.

"This right here is the dope before we cut it. It's the shit that you and your friend brought back. I'm gonna show you how to cut it with the quad 9 and bonita. Grab a pair of gloves and a mask off the counter," he said, putting on the gloves.

Chastity did as she was told, while he grabbed one of the keys. He spent the next three hours showing her how to cut, wrap, and seal the product. She caught on quick and was doing it by herself after a couple of tries. They had turned one key into 10. They only bagged a quarter of one up into bundles.

"Do you have a name to call your work?" Chris asked.

"No."

"Well, I think we should put our old brand on it to build your clientele up. Trust me… when they see this name back on the streets, you will be shutting everybody else down."

"What name is that?' Chastity asked excitedly.

Chris went over to his computer and started typing on the key pad. After he was finished, he opened the floor safe and grabbed some paper out, inserting it into the printer. Once he printed out the logo, he passed it to Chastity so she could see.

"This is the name of your product. I didn't think that we would ever be using this name again, but this will be your way to state your claim on these streets.

"'Numbers'! When I was little, I used to see these bags laying on the street as I walked to school. This was yours?" Chastity asked.

No, that era belonged to my brother. After he retired from the game, I took over. I never sold my shit under that brand because I wanted to establish my own name. Since you are gonna be running shit, I want you to use that name until you're able to hold your own. If you get into any kind of drama, you call me ASAP, and I will send some people over to you. Do you have a couple of people that you trust to put on your team, or do you want me to hire someone?"

"What will they be doing?"

"Cutting, bagging, and branding the bags. I have a lot of shit for you to get out on the streets if you're ready."

"Yeah, my best friend and her sisters will do it. I'll call her and let her know," Chastity said, excited that she was about to make some money.

They were wrapping their meeting up when Chris said, "Oh, yeah, before I take you back home, I have to show you one more thing. Follow me."

He led her into the basement of the house. When they got there, he clicked the light switch 10 times, and then put the switch between the off and on position, signaling the wall to slide open. Chastity was shocked at what she saw. There had to be at least a hundred guns hanging throughout the wall and setting on the room's two tables.

"This is the house armory. If you ever feel the need to handle something, just grab what you need to eliminate the problem. Word of advice... never be contrite about anything you do. In order to be successful and stay ahead in this game, sometimes you have to alleviate the problem all together.

Never get caught up in the shenanigans and always stay one step ahead of the competition," Chris said, as he closed the wall by clicking the switch twice and leaving it in the off position.

"How will I get around with no car to drive?'

"We are going to meet my wife, and she gonna take you over to my lot and give you a car. It should be ready for you by now, so let's go before she thinks we're doing something," he said smiling.

As they headed for the door, Chris' phone rang. "That's her now, she's outside. I have some other business to take care of, but she will take you. Don't forget that you will be going to Tampa Bay this time instead of Miami. Your plane will be leaving at 3:00 p.m. tomorrow from Gate B, so don't be late!"

"I won't and thank you for everything that you're doing for me," she said, walking out through the door and getting in the Benz with Chris's wife, Nyia.

Chris went around to the driver's side and gave his wife a kiss. He then jumped in his car and pulled out right behind them. Now that Numbers was back on the street, he knew it was only a matter of time that every block would be pumping uncontrollable amounts of heroin. He could retire his brand and enjoy sitting back just like E.J. was doing.

* * *

Rudy was sitting outside, enjoying the breeze, and watching to see who was on the block. Since they moved into the apartment, they never had the chance to meet their neighbors. Her real intention was to see what niggas was getting money around there.

While she was sitting on the step, a guy in an Infiniti Jeep pulled up. He got out of the truck and walked into the apartment next to hers. He wasn't cute but he had a lot of jewelry, which made Rudy want him. When he came back out, Rudy and he talked to each other.

Before she had the chance to say anything else, a female and two little boys came out and headed for the truck.

"Damn, that must be his family. Oh well, I guess I'll have to become a home wrecker 'cause I'm going to snatch and juice his ass," she said to herself, laughing at her own joke.

"Bottle after bottle, drink until I overdose. Pull up in a Phantom; watch these bitches catch the Holy Ghost. Every time I step up in the dealer, I be going broke . . ." Meek Mill and Drake blasted through the speakers, causing Rudy to look up.

When she saw who was parking, she smiled and stood up. "Where the hell you get this car from?"

Chastity stepped out of the candy apple red Cadillac SRX and walked over to her friend.

"I told you that we were going to make some money, which is exactly what we're about to do. I have to grab something real quick from inside the apartment. Call Kita, Sharon, and Neatra, and tell them to be home by the time we get there. It's time to get at this money," Chastity said, running into the building.

When she came back out, she and Rudy jumped into the car and headed for south Philly. Chastity let Rudy drive so she could become familiar with the car. She took the information from Chris and locked it into her memory. Once she filled in her friends as to what was up, she was sure that they would be on the team. Chastity cranked the music up as they jumped on the expressway.

* * *

"All I need you to do is cut the dope, package it, and put the name on it. Each of you will make $1,000 a week, and you get two days off. If you choose to stay longer, you will definitely benefit from it tremendously. It's a lot of work

128

y'all, I'm not gonna lie. I'm asking for your help so that y'all can eat like me. Kita, your job pays you almost that every two weeks. Just think about all the extra money you will have to spend!" Chastity said, looking at the girls for confirmation.

"Sharon and Neatra, y'all already know the deal about the streets because both of you have boyfriends that deal dope."

"Kita does too," Neatra said.

"Yeah, but Kita's man only sells coke. If she talks him into buying dope from us though, she will benefit from that. Anyway, Rudy... you're my best friend, so if you're not with me, I don't want to do it at all. Y'all are my family. As a matter of fact, the only family I have. When we lock these streets down and blow up, I promise everyone will get more," Chastity said sincerely.

"Chas, count me in," Rudy said.

"Me, too," Kita said.

Neatra and Sharon looked at each other and both nodded their heads. Just like that, their bond was formed.

"So what's the name of our dope we putting out there?" Rudy asked, as everyone sat down onto the couch.

"It's called Numbers, and once people see that it's back, it should blow up Chris told me," Chastity said.

"When do we start hugging that shit up? If I'm quitting my job, I might as well start my new one ASAP," Kita said, as they all laughed.

"Let's go get started then. I have to go out of town tomorrow by myself," Chastity said, looking at Rudy. "But when I get back, I'll take y'all around, showing y'all who gets what and the amount they owe. We are going to start cutting the dope tonight, so Kita, follow me and Rudy to the spot."

They all jumped in the two cars and headed over to Reno Street to start the process of making money.

"Rudy, you are my right hand, so you will be putting the bundles out on the blocks starting tonight. I want to have some of our clientele established by the time I return. I don't want to wait until I get back. After we bag some of it up, we're gonna deliver it," Chastity said, as they headed to west Philly.

"Let's get this money then."

* * *

Mal and Reese were leaving Scooter's Sports Bar on 38th and Lancaster Avenue, when Mal's cell phone rang.

"What's up, Ant?" Mal said, getting in the car.

"Yo, we need some more chicken and not from the store you got the last pack from. That shit was spoiled," Ant said.

Mal knew that Ant was talking about dope. That was the code name everybody used to avoid incriminating anybody.

"We are working on something, and I'll get back to you in the morning to let you know."

"Alright, I'll holla at you then," Ant said, ending the call.

"Yo, we need to find us a plug quick. Nobody wants that garbage we've been selling. Niggas really gonna start sliding out of town to get shit," Mal told Reese.

"Well, tomorrow we gonna have to go out of town and rob us a couple of niggas. We can bring the work back and sell it to our workers.'

"That's a good plan, but let's do it like we did when Hakeem was home. That way works much better. The only problem is finding a bitch to roll with us on our mission. Who is a rider like that?" Mal asked quizzically.

"I know the perfect girl. I'm about to call her now and see if we can link up. She about her bread, so I know she will roll with us," Reese said, as they rode past 39th and Fairmont.

They saw at least 15 fiends out copping from a couple of niggas. "I wonder what kind of dope they got," Mal said.

Reese pulled over and stopped one of the fiends before they went into their crib.

"What's the name of that dope? I'm trying to find some," Reese asked, as if he was a crack head.

"Numbers!" the crack head said, all excited. "They got Numbers back on the street. This is the best dope ever."

Reese and Mal looked at each other. They remembered how that drug had the whole tristate area and more popping. Now they had to find out who brought it back because they wanted in.

"This chick just texted me saying I could come through so I'm gonna head over there after I drop you off. Tomorrow, we're gonna get a plug with that Numbers shit," Reese said, heading for Mal's crib.

"Yeah, that's if they want to deal with us. It seems like Hakeem got everybody against us since we burnt him on that cash.

"Fuck that, we need to get paid, so if I have to get on my knees and beg, then fuck it. If that don't work, then we kill his ass," Reese said smirking.

He dropped Mal off and headed over to Rudy's crib.

* * *

It was 4:35 a.m. and Reese had just finished up fucking Rudy for the second time. He was lying in the bed thinking about how he was gonna be able to link up with whoever had that powerful dope back out on the streets. He saw firsthand how pure that shit was from when he and Keem used to sell if for some dude before he was murdered.

"What are you thinking about?" Rudy asked while rubbing his dick.

"Shit, I have to find me a new connect and fast. My product is not as it used to be. If I can find one though, I can get back to this money."

"What happened to the people that y'all were dealing with?"

Reese just sighed, "Everyone Hakeem got snatched up. We haven't been able to find a plug. Now we're selling bullshit, while someone has that Numbers dope poppin' again. It's not telling when that shit will take Philly over again."

Rudy sat there thinking if she should tell him that it was her and Chastity that just put that shit back in the streets tonight. From what he said, that shit was already starting to blow up again.

She decided not to say anything until she talked to Chastity about it first. If he need a plug, it was gonna be them.

"Well, I hope you do find one so you won't have to be all stressed out," Rudy said.

"Why don't you give me one more of those famous blow jobs before I get up out of here," he said, as he pushed her head down towards his dick.

"I got you," Rudy told him, as she took his semi erect penis into her mouth.

EIGHTEEN

THE NEXT MORNING, CHASTITY woke up to the door buzzer. She turned over in an attempt to return back to sleep, but it wasn't working. She got up and threw on a pair of shorts before going to answer the door.

She opened the door and saw the deliveryman standing in the doorway holding a large box in his hands.

"I have a delivery for Ms. Chastity Davis," he said, passing her the box.

She signed for it and passed the clipboard back to the guy, as he left without even asking for a tip. Chastity walked back into her room and sat on her bed. When she opened the card, it read:

To a very special woman:

Ever since that day I saw you at the club, I wanted to reach out to you. Since you don't want to be showered with expensive gifts, I thought that I'd sent you something not so expensive. Happy birthday, Chastity.

Truly yours, E.J.

A smile came across her face as she opened the box to see two dozen long-stem roses. They were beautiful and special to her because no one had ever done something so simple like that for her. There was a ribbon wrapped around it that read, "Make a wish and it might come true."

"She set the flowers down and walked into the bathroom to pee. She was about to text Rudy when her phone rang. The caller I.D. showed that it was Chris.

"Hello."

"Chastity, how are things going with you?"

"Everything is good. We put some product out last night, and it sold like candy. They ran out before 1:00 this morning, so we dropped more off."

"That's good to hear, but there's been a slight change of plans for your trip to Tampa," Chris said.

"What happened? I'm listening," she said, thinking she wouldn't be able to make any money

"You're still going to go, but it's not for the stuff we talked about. You have to be at the airport by 2:00 p.m. this afternoon. You're not flying on a commercial airline. You will be on a private jet. There is a private air hangar before you get to Terminal F. The jet is called One Flight International, and the pilot is Walter."

"So, I'll still be going by myself?"

"Yes, so have fun, okay. A car will be waiting once you're flight lands in Tampa. I will help Rudy with the distribution of the work today. Call me when you return," Chris said, ending the call.

Chastity finished using the bathroom, and then took as shower. After dressing, she called Rudy and told her to come home so that she could drop her off at the airport by 1:00 p.m.

Rudy told her that she would be there in 20 minutes because she had to talk to her anyway. She put the roses in a vase and set it on her dresser, made something to eat, and waited for Rudy.

* * *

Hakeem had just gotten off the phone with Meka. She told him that she didn't want to raise a baby by herself, so she got an abortion. He was so heated that he wanted to be left alone. He returned to his cell and found his cellmate reading his mail.

"What the fuck are you doing in my shit?" he said, startling the dude, as he jumped up with the letter still in his hand.

"I, I, I'm sorry! I was just reading your letter that was on my bed. I thought you wanted me to read it."

"Hakeem was so pissed off about the phone call that he forgot that he asked his neighbor to throw the letter on the bed in his cell.

"Nigga, you know that shit wasn't yours. So why did you touch it?" he said, as he shut the door behind him.

"I already told you it was on my bunk, so I assumed you wanted me to read it. My fault, dog."

"Fuck all that, nigga, strap up."

"So you want to fight over some bullshit misconception, huh?" the dude said, putting on his shoes.

Hakeem needed to release some tension; so before the dude could put on his other shoe, he kneed him in the mouth. The dude fell backwards, and Hakeem started swinging hang maker after hang maker, connecting with every blow.

All the dude could do was grab Hakeem and try to slam him. The room was too big, so Hakeem was able to adjust to his wrestling. He pushed him back and they went blow for blow, with both men drawing blood.

The fight lasted for five minutes before a couple of inmates broke it up.

"You better not be in here when I come back pussy, or we gonna rumble the whole time we're locked in," Hakeem said, as two of his boys pulled him out of the cell.

The dude was no bitch, but he didn't want that kind of drama, so he changed his blood shirt and packed his shit. He went up the correctional officer's desk and told her that he wanted to check in (to protective custody). She called for a sergeant and they escorted him over to B-block.

Hakeem, still heated about his phone call, went in the yard and sat in the corner by himself wondering who he was gonna get to beat the shit out of Meka for killing his child.

* * *

135

The jet landed in Tampa Bay around 4:00 p.m. When Chastity stepped off the jet, she saw the most beautiful car she had ever laid eyes on waiting for her. It was a 2014 English white and diamond black Rolls Royce Wraith. She never in her life imagined that she would be riding in something so expensive and it wasn't even a dream. The chauffer opened the door for her, as she sat in the comfortable seat. He hopped in and pulled off.

"Mr. Johnson is waiting for you at the restaurant. We will be there in about 45 minutes. You can sit back and watch television if you like. The screen is voice activated and you can access Netflix or the internet. If you don't wish to do that, you can listen to some music. The choice is yours," he said.

Chastity couldn't believe all the features this car had. She relaxed and listened to Alicia Keys, until she drifted off to sleep on the plush seats.

"Some people live for the fortune; some people live for the fame. Some people live for the power, yeah; some people live just to play the game. . ."

* * *

Chastity woke up just in time to see the driver pull up to an extravagant restaurant. When he let her out, E.J. was standing at the door waiting for her.

"It's nice to see you again," he said, giving her a hug and kiss on the cheek.

Chastity couldn't help but to get a good whiff of the Valentino Uomo cologne he was wearing. She had to admit that he was looking good.

"Why did you fly me out here without having me take anything back with me?"

"Oh, but you see, you will be taking something back with you. Let's go inside and talk. It's too hot out here for me," E.J. said, leading her to a table in the back.

They sat down and the waitress came over and took their order.

"What would you like to drink, sir?" she asked.

"I'll have a sparkling rosé lemonade, and the lady will have?"

"A club soda. Thank you," Chastity said.

"I'll be right back with your drinks," she said, walking off and leaving the two of them to talk.

Chastity waited to see if he would be the first to break the silence, but when he didn't she began, she said, "So what will I be taking back?"

"Knowledge… and a better understanding of the game that you so desperately want to be apart of. See, Chastity, even though I'm retired, I still have a grasp on everything that goes on. You're using a brand name that I spilled blood to uphold. Once you put that name on the streets, you will inherit everything that comes with it. Are you ready for that?"

"Yes, I've been ready," Chastity responded.

"You're going to rise to the top faster than you could ever imagine. A couple of months from now, when you think about what you had to do to get where you are, your self-esteem grows. All the obstacles you've had to overcome are more indicative of your level of success than the position that you will hold. Don't let the fame and fortune make you bigheaded, because just as fast as you got it, you could lose it in a blink of an eye. Are we clear so far?"

Chastity nodded her head in agreement and continued to listen to everything E.J. said. They talked and ate for three hours. He told her so much that she didn't want to leave. She wanted to continue learning more and more from this man.

They left the restaurant, and instead of taking the Rolls Royce, they hopped in E.J.'s new toy. It was a pearl white convertible Maserati Ghibli S Q4. Chastity thought the Rolls was hot. That didn't have anything on this car.

She got in, and waited for him to get in the driver's side. Once they pulled off, she said, "Do you always try to impress girls like this?"

E.J. laughed. "No, I don't try to impress anybody. I'm very, very blessed right now, and I don't mind sharing."

"So where is your girl at?"

"I don't have one anymore. I've been determined to find someone special, but that time hasn't yet come."

"Never married?"

"Yes, actually I was, but now I'm divorced. It's a long story that I don't want to discuss right now."

They drove to the 11000 block of Florida Avenue where E.J. stopped at a closed car dealership. He beeped his horn and a white man came out. He handed E.J. some paperwork, and then jumped in his car and left.

E.J. pulled off, noticing Chastity staring at him. He said, "That was the man who sold me this car. I had to pick up the papers."

"I didn't say anything," she said smiling.

"I'm gonna take you to my place so that you can freshen up before we hit the club. I know that you're tired from the flight, long drive, and my continuous chatter," he said.

Chastity smiled at him again and then relaxed. She was starting to like him, but she didn't want to let the cat out of the bag just yet. She wanted to see how the rest of the night went. She only could stay for a day or two before she had to get back to Philly to help her team. While she was here, though, she was going to soak it all up.

* * *

They both were lounging in one of E.J.'s clubs in Tampa, having a good time, when the DJ said, "Let's give a happy belated birthday wish to a really beautiful lady, Ms. Chastity Davis."

Everyone in the crowded tipped their glasses up towards Chastity and said, "Happy birthday."

She was awe-struck from all of the attention she was receiving. After greeting her, everyone in the club went back to dancing and enjoying their night.

"You seem to be a very important man everywhere we go. Let me guess, this is another one of your establishments?" she whispered in his ear over the loud music that was playing.

"You're absolutely correct. I own two clubs in five different cities... and counting. My plan is to have a club in every city on the East coast. Then I can move on to the West coast as well," he said.

"Someone's going to be very busy."

"Don't worry. I'll never be too busy for you. You will always have my undivided attention, even when you're miles away."

Chastity could only blush at the way he was always prepared for anything she said. As they sat and talked about any and everything, the more their attention for one another grew. They stayed at the club until 1:00 in the morning dancing and having a good time, before leaving to head back to E.J.'s estate.

"You don't have to stay at the hotel that I arranged for you. I have plenty of rooms for you here," E.J. said, getting out of the car.

At first, Chastity was skeptical about staying there, but then realized that he had been the perfect gentleman the whole night. Besides, she wanted to stay there with him anyway.

They sat in the living room and continued to talk about different subjects. The more they talked, the smarter Chastity became. There was a lot of sexual tension between them, but neither one acted on it yet. They each waited for the other to make the first move.

139

Tired of the waiting game E.J. leaned over and took her lips into his mouth, kissing her seductively. His hands caressed her body until they reached her round ass, squeezing it tightly. He was so hard that she could feel it through his pants, as he laid her back on the couch, positioning himself between her legs.

They were in pure heat as he leaned up and slid his hand up her dress. Her clit was throbbing for attention, as he slid her thong to the side and played with it. She was in so much pleasure that she came before he even had the chance to do anything else.

He removed his hand and then put it in her mouth, letting her taste her own juices. E.J. started licking her inner thighs, slowly tongue kissing her clitoris. He made love to her clit with his tongue, until her juices started flowing into his mouth.

After he pleased her, she wanted to reciprocate the favor. She stood up and pushed him back on the couch. She scooted down in between his legs and pulled his off pants and boxers. Chastity knew that her head game was better than the porn star Superhead, so it wasn't a surprise when he began having convulsions while she put her head game down.

E.J. felt himself about to erupt, so he tried to pull his dick out of her mouth. She wouldn't let him though. He shot his load down her throat.

"Damn, girl, you are the best," he said panting.

"Oh, I'm not done yet. You have a bitch ready to fuck all night."

"Follow me then," he said, leading her upstairs to his bedroom.

When they reached his room, he lifted her dress over her head and was completely shocked by the flawless beauty that stood before him. They walked over to the bed and Chastity laid down, without her eyes ever breaking from his.

"The first time I saw your face, I knew that we belonged together. I couldn't tell you then because you were with someone."

Chastity put her finger over his lips, silencing what he was saying, "I'm not with him anymore. I'm here with you. So what does it mean?"

"I'll tell you what it means after we make passionate love," he said, as he stood up on his knees and grabbed his erection.

Chastity grabbed it and started rubbing the tip all over her clit, up and down and side to side. When he finally entered her hot, wet pussy, she arched her back, letting out a moan, while he took her to complete ecstasy.

He gave her long, hard strokes, while pushing her legs over her head, so that he could go deeper and deeper inside of her.

"That's it, baby," give it to me," she said, synchronizing her rhythm with his

By the time they grew tired from all the lovemaking, it was 6:00 a.m. They fell asleep, cuddled in each other's arms.

* * *

Chastity woke up to an empty bed. She looked at the clock and saw that it was 2:00 in the afternoon. She sat up and saw the massive size of the bedroom. Every part of it screamed money and power. She went to use the bathroom, when her phone started ringing.

"Hey, sexy," the male voice said.

"Hello to you. I just woke up and noticed that you weren't here," Chastity replied, already knowing who it was.

"You know what they say: the early bird catches the worm. Is there anything you would like to do today?"

"Hmmmm, let me think, besides getting some more of that good loving from last night. I did want to do a little shopping before I head back to Philly," she answered, sitting on the toilet.

"Do you have to go back today?"

"Yes, but I can come back in a couple of weeks. I have a business that needs my full attention right now, just like you have priorities that you need to get in order."

"Okay, I guess you're right. Well, you can go into my garage and take whatever car you want to do your shopping. The keys are in the ignition. I'll be home before you leave, so that I can take you to the tarmac personally and see you off."

"Well, I will only be a few hours. I'll have to punch a mall in on the GPS because I don't know where the hell I'm going. See you when you get home," she said, before ending the call.

She took a quick shower, dressed, and headed for the garage. When she opened the door, she damn near passed out at the sight of all the exclusive vehicles lined up. There had to be at least 15 of them, and they all looked like they just came off the showroom floor.

There was a 2014 Lamborghini Huracán and a Lamborghini Roadster, same year. He also owned a 2003 Ferrari Enzo, a 2009 Porsche Carrera GT, a 2011 black-on-black Maybach, and a 2009 Koenigsegg CCXR. To top it off, he even had a 2014 Toyota Tundra Devolro that had bulletproof armor and windows, just in case he had beef. Those were just some of his many toys sitting around. Outside in the driveway sat four of his motorcycles, including a 2013 Harley-Davidson, a 2014 Yamaha 1100, a Honda CBR, and a 1999 Ducati 1199 Superleggera.

Chastity didn't know which one she wanted to take, so she chose the 2012 Mercedes McLaren. It was an all-red two-seater. She set her purse on the passenger seat, and then went back into the house to change her panties. She smiled because the excitement of all the cars had caused her to orgasm.

LOST AND TURNED OUT

NINETEEN

TWO DAYS HAD PASSED since Reese and Mal had talked to a dealer who said that he would contact his supplier and see if he could help with their situation. They finally received the call they were expecting. Now both men were sitting inside of the Old Country Buffet waiting for the chance to meet their soon-to-be supplier.

"Why did we have to come to this fucking restaurant instead of some other one in the hood? I hate these Upper Darby cops," Mal said.

They were on 69th Street in Upper Darby. They hated the fact that they were right down the street from the police station. Just when Reese was about to respond to his friend, two females and a dude walked into the place. They looked in Reese and Mal's direction, and then they walked towards their table.

"What the hell is she here for?" Reese asked, referring to Rudy.

"They're coming towards us. I guess your little jump-off wants to say hi," Mal said smirking

Chastity, Rudy, and Chris came over and sat down next to them. Chastity was the first to speak.

"Reese, Mal... I like y'all to meet Chris. Chris, this is Reese and Mal. I know you're probably wondering why we're here, so let me save you the trouble of asking. We are gonna be your new connects. Numbers is my responsibility now, which means I'm the HBIC (Head Bitch in Charge) of this operation," Chastity said, with authority in her voice.

"Get the fuck out of here. This must be some kind of joke. Tell me that this is a joke, right?" Reese said.

"This is no joke. You will be dealing with Rudy or me. When you come to re-up, please come correct. Reese and Mal, I really need both of you to be on my team. You will definitely reap the benefits if you do. Not only will you be copping from me, you would also be my muscle. I really don't need you for it, but because you are from our hood, I need hood soldiers."

"Wait, wait, wait a fucking minute," Reese said, looking at Chris. "You mean to tell me that these two little fucking girls are big-time suppliers in the city? They are the ones responsible for Numbers? I can't believe it."

Chris was about to say something but was interrupted by Rudy. "Well, believe it. You said a couple of days ago that you needed a better supplier, so here we are making you the deal of a lifetime. Take it or leave it. The choice is yours to make."

"Before you make that choice, I want you to know that these girls are about to take over the whole East coast, so it would be smart to make the right decision. I supplied your friend Hakeem for a very long time, and now you have the chance to get with a team that, without a doubt, will take over every city around here, "Chris said.

Mal and Reese contemplated the decision that would ultimately change their lives. They wanted the work, but they didn't feel right taking it from a 17-year-old girl. Mal was wondering how the hell she gained so much power in this little bit of time. *She must be fucking him,* he thought.

"Give us a day to think about it, if you don't mind. Can we still cop a few bundles for now?" Mal asked.

"Yeah; although we'll do you one better. We'll give you fifty bundles, and you can get back to us when you're done," Chastity said, sitting like a true boss.

"That'll work," Reese said.

"Rudy will call you in about an hour to pick the work up. I'll see you later, gentlemen," Chastity said, pulling out a hundred dollar bill and placing it on the table, as they walked out the door.

"What the fuck just happened here? This bitch is a fucking boss, or is she just fucking him?" Reese said.

"I don't know, but let's go throw some salt in the face of Hakeem and see what his reaction will be," Mal said.

They weren't dealing with Keem anymore since he wouldn't hook them up with the connect, so they decided to send a birdie out to him that his ex was now a boss.

* * *

After the meeting, Chastity left the restaurant and, along with Rudy, headed to the spot on Reno Street.

"Did you see the looks on their faces when you told them who the boss was behind Numbers?" Rudy said.

"Hell yeah, and I don't think they like it either. Their pride will likely get in the way of them making money, but I hope they will consider my offer. That's why I'm going to give them the work, just to see if they will join the team."

"Well, after we leave the crib, let's catch the salon on 52nd Street and get our nails done. Look at my shit, they are past due."

"Well, they are going to have to wait until tomorrow, 'cause we're going to be working our asses off tonight to get more of this product out," Chastity replied.

Rudy wanted to protest, but thought better of it. She knew that in order to control the streets, she had to sacrifice some things.

When they arrived at the stash spot, Kita and Neatra were already bagging the product. Chastity didn't worry about them stealing anything because she had cameras everywhere. Some were visible and others weren't. That way if something came up missing, she would know, because she and Chris were the only ones that knew where the hidden cameras were.

"Damn, what time did y'all get here? That's a lot of work done already," Rudy said, as they walked into the kitchen.

"Time is money, and I'm not trying to waste any," Kita answered, not taking her eyes off of her work.

Chastity and Rudy put their gloves and masks on, and they joined the girls so that they could get at least a half on the streets tonight.

"Did Sharon already come past here?" Chastity questioned.

"Yep, the work is on its way to Reese and Mal now. She grabbed fifty bundles. I also gave her a hundred bundles to drop off in north Philly and another hundred for the south Philly spot. Is that good enough?" Neatra asked.

"Great! Now all we will have to do is drop off the work in Delaware tomorrow morning," Chastity replied.

They spent the next four hours bagging up dope and readying for the distribution in the morning. When they left from the spot, everybody was so tired that they all stayed at Chastity and Rudy's apartment because it was closer than driving to south Philly.

* * *

Chastity drove out to Delaware the next morning, while Rudy traveled to the other spots in Jersey. She was looking for someone who used to work for some dude named Scrap. Scrap was one of the people killed in a shoot-out a couple of years ago back when Numbers was nationwide. Chris had sent her out there, because once they had Delaware back in play, other states would follow.

When she pulled up to 3rd and Harrison, she saw a couple of niggas chillin' on the steps. She rolled down the passenger-side window when she stopped in front of the group.

"Any of your names Dep or Curt?"

One of the dudes stood up and came over to the window. He scooted down and looked into the car at the beautiful woman sitting in the driver's seat. His eyes never left her pussy, as he could see her lips poking out through the tights she was wearing.

"What's up, ma? Why you looking for me?" Curt asked.

"First of all, what's your name, because I asked for either or. Secondly, when you talk to me, look at my face not my pussy, because you'll never get to see the real thing," she said, with an attitude.

"Never say never. Anyway, my name is Curt, but everybody calls me Cocaine. Is there something that you need?"

"Get in the car. I want to talk to you for a minute."

Curt hopped in the car and Chastity pulled around the corner so that they could chat. "Do you remember the dope Numbers?" She asked once she parked.

"What about it?"

"I'm trying to put it back on these streets. I know you've been selling Chris' product, but he wants me to take over. My product is going to be the same time, but a little more pure, just as it used to be. I need some strong soldiers to make it work. Are you down or what?"

Curt thought about how it would feel to fuck her, but then he started thinking about the money. Numbers would boost his already pumping block to a super pumping block. Once they saw that it was back, business would be at an all-time high.

"How much could you get me today?" he asked.

"How much are you willing to buy right now?"

"I could use a thousand bundles if the price is right," he said, now looking at her face instead of between her thighs.

"Okay, I'll give that to you for $28,000. Give me $14,000 up front and I'll pick up the rest in a couple of days. Don't try any treachery shit because I'm a girl, because *that* my friend will get you bodied. I'm the real deal, not a flunky; so if you're loyal, then you will blow up with me. Are we clear on that?"

"That's cool. So when will I have my product?"

"How fast can you get my money?' she countered.

"I'll have it by this evening, if you come back at 5:00. Maybe I could even take you out to eat or something," he said, trying his hand.

"Sorry, cutie, but I'm taken; besides, based on the way that little skinny girl is looking at us, she must be your girlfriend."

Curt looked up at a girl standing on the corner and he could see that she was ready to beat his and Chastity's asses.

"I have to go, but 5:00 will be good," he said, jumping out of the car and running over to the girl.

Chastity pulled out laughing as the girl began cursing and hitting him, as they walked up the street.

"One down, a couple more to go," she said to herself, as she went to find Dep and another dude named Big B.

* * *

Hakeem was heated when he got the news about Chastity and Chris. He read the letter two more times from some bitch who lived in the projects. Everybody had left him for dead when they found out he got 20 years. It was his fault about Chastity because he was the one that the told her to roll. He was mad at his so-called boys for committing larceny against him.

It seemed as if everyone was trying to humiliate him in some shape, form, or fashion. Once he got out of there, he made a promise to himself that he was going to release some excruciating pain, starting with Chris and his boys.

Right now, it was time for dinner, so he got out of his bunk and went to grab his tray from the block workers. After dinner, he was going to get on the phone and see what else he could find out about the streets.

TWENTY

IT HAD BEEN MONTHS now since Chastity had linked up with the out-of-town workers in Delaware and New Jersey. She had the streets on lock now, and everybody was copping from her because of the name on her product. Now, instead of the one stash house, she was using three. They even had to hire a couple more people to help bag up the work. She took advice from her now boyfriend, E.J., to keep the women in the house with only panties on while working.

She went down to Florida every chance she could get so that she could be with E.J. It grew to the point where she didn't have to pack an overnight bag because she had a closet and dresser full of clothes there. E.J. was slowly trying to move her in, but she wouldn't let him.

She always tried to get him to come to Philly, but he would easily decline the offer. The long distance relationship was good for both of them, but there were times when they wanted to be near each other, but couldn't. He didn't have to give her anything because she was making so much money that she and her friends would be up all night counting. E.J. helped her get an offshore account to put in most of the money so that if they ever got popped, the feds wouldn't be able to touch it.

Chastity and Rudy were leaving the Olive Garden on City Line Avenue when a green Ford Taurus pulled up beside them. It was tinted out so they couldn't see who was inside.

The passenger rolled down the window and Chastity looked to see who it was. Her mouth dropped open when she saw her Uncle Tony in the passenger seat. He had some young girl driving. She looked as if she was only 16 years old.

"What do you want, Uncle Tony? Why do you have that little-ass girl in the car with you?" Chastity asked.

"Don't worry about that. I'm hearing that you are the person to see in these streets right now. So what are you out here doing?" he countered.

"What I do is none of your business; and unless you want your shit all over the streets, I suggest you and your little friend keep it moving."

Her uncle stared at her for a few minutes before saying, "Whenever you're ready to come home, I'll be waiting."

They pulled off, leaving them standing there. Chastity was heated, and it was time for him to get a taste of his own medicine. She had a trick up her sleeve for him. The time was approaching at a rapid pace.

"Ohhhh, I can't stand his molesting ass. He will pay for this shit if it's the last thing I do on this earth," Chastity said.

"Don't worry about his ass, we have money to collect. So let's head out to Delaware and pick it up," Rudy replied.

"You're right, plus I have to get ready so that I can fly down to Florida in a couple of days."

"I'm going with you this time. You're not leaving me here with Sharon and Neatra. I'm sure there are some sexy niggas out there willing to keep me company while you and your boo have fun."

"We'll see. Let's swing past Reese and Mal's crib first, and see what's going on with that money. From there, we can hit the expressway and visit+ our Delaware workers," Chastity said, as they jumped in her car and headed to see Reese.

* * *

After picking up the money from Reese and Mal, Chastity headed out to Delaware to see how Big B, Curt, and Dep made out. She had given each of them a thousand bundles to do as they pleased, as long as they had her $28,000 when she came for it.

When she pulled up to 3rd and Harrison, she didn't see Curt or Dep, but Big B was out there grinding. She beeped the horn as Rudy rolled down the window, and Big B walked over the car.

"What's good, Chas? Damn, who is this with you?" he said, looking at Rudy.

"Your boss, nigga! Now do you have that paper for us?" Rudy asked.

Big B was at a loss for words. He signaled one of the niggas to come over. The young boy came over with a bag in his hand. He passed it to Big B and went back to work

"This is your 28 rocks right here. I need more work today because this shit is flowing crazy out here," Big B said, passing the bag to Rudy.

Chastity hit the secret code to the stash box and pulled out a hundred bundles for him. She placed the money into it without even counting it because they all had a level of understanding. If that money comes up short, somebody is gonna bleed.

"Here you go, B. I'll see you in a couple of days. If you get low, hit my phone and somebody will be here to see you."

"Where are Curt and Dep at?" Rudy questioned.

"They are both handling shit over on New Castle Avenue. They have that shit doing twice the numbers that it was. If you leave now you can catch the rush and see for yourself," Big B told them.

They pulled off, leaving Big B to return to grinding. They called Brandon, Big B, because he was a big nigga and he wouldn't hesitate to put his murder game down. Chastity put him on the team because she knew he could hold his own.

Curt on the other hand, was a livewire that could explode at any given time if provoked. He stayed strapped with big shit, and he loved selling coke to rich white people. That's where he earned the name Cocaine.

Dep was a silent assassin. He was the low-key one of the three. People would think that he was a pussy because he never got into a confrontation, but he was the last person who you would want to try. He didn't carry guns because he had to see his parole officer every week, and he didn't know when he would show up. When the time came for him to go to war though, all types of shit would come out, from AR-15s to rocket launchers. He had a connect at the Dover Military Base, so whatever he needed; he got dirt-cheap.

Chastity and Rudy pulled up on New Castle Avenue looking for Dep and Curt. Just as Big B said, all they had to do was follow the crowd of fiends, and they would see them. She pulled over and beeped the horn; at the same time, her cell phone rang. She looked at the caller ID and it was Dep. They saw Chastity's car so he hung up.

He walked up to the car, with Curt right behind him. "Damn man, you're gonna live a long time. I was just calling you because we only have a couple of bags left. Tell us you have a re-up for me," Dep said, leaning on the car.

"As long as you have that paper for me," Chastity said.

Curt ran over to the trunk of his Dodge Magnum and grabbed the bag with the money in it. Rudy hit the sequence of functions causing the stash box to open once more. She took out 2,000 bundles and put the money that Curt passed her into it before closing it up.

"That is a hundred a piece in there. I know y'all might need more but that's all we brought for now. Call if you run low before we come back out here. We also dropped off a hundred to Big B, so y'all should be straight for a couple of days," Rudy told them.

"Good looking, and if y'all need us, we're only a phone call away," Curt said, still trying to flirt, even though he knew that he didn't have a chance.

"Come on, man, let's get back to this group. You're always trying to mack something. See y'all later," Dep said, as they headed back over to the crib to finish trapping.

"Time to get back to Philly and count this money. I hope it's all there, because I would hate to send the boys back out here on some rah, rah shit!' Chastity said, as they pulled off.

They were heading back to Philly, but the whole time they didn't even know that they were being followed. Reese and some nigga who was a stick-up kid from north Philly named Marv had been watching them since they left.

"Yo, I told you this would be an easy hit. I want to you to handle it, and I'll split it with you and whomever you get. Just be careful because they have some heavy hitters that's sponsoring them. That's why I can't be seen helping you," Reese said.

"I got this, but who do you want me to hit first, those Delaware niggas or the bitches?"

"Get the bitches first because they carry the most money. I want it all, you feel me? If Mal says anything to you, you don't know me. He likes dealing with them, I don't."

"What is your problem with them, you never told me."

"Don't worry about that. Just handle your part of the deal and I'll handle mine," Reese said, as they headed back.

Reese despised Chastity because she was where he wanted to be. He decided to rob them; and if they refused to give up the cash, then they would pay with their lives. He continued pretending to be a part of the team so he could get close to them without them knowing all the envy that he had towards them. He thought that the time was right for his flunky to strike, so he told him to handle it that night.

* * *

Later that night, Chastity left the stash spot to return home. Rudy stayed with Kita so they could bag up a little longer. Chastity hopped in her car and threw the bag with the $82,000 in it in the back seat. Before she went home, she wanted some seafood, so she swung by Bottom of the Sea in west Philly.

When she parked, she ran into the store to grab her platter that she had already called in. After paying for her food, she walked out and headed for her car. It was dark in the parking lot so she never saw the two niggas in all black creeping up on her.

As soon as she reached her car, they both jumped out on her aiming their guns. "Bitch, you scream and you die!"

Chastity froze up and couldn't move. They pushed her over the hood of the car, looking for the keys.

"Grab the bag in the back seat," one of the assailants told the other.

He grabbed the bag and shut the door. Chastity had tears coming down her face. She was so careless tonight and now it was going to cost her. She looked around hoping someone would help her, but there was no one in sight.

"Let's have some fun with this bitch. Look at the ass on her. I know that pussy is good," one dude said.

"Please don't hurt me. I won't say anything," Chastity said, wondering what they were about to do to her.

"If you cooperate, we'll let you go. Move over to that empty lot right there, and don't even think about screaming," the dude said.

Another girl unknowingly watched the robbery while she sat in her car, also waiting for her food. She chose to not intervene until they started forcing her into the dark lot. She jumped out the car and crept up behind them, trying to be inconspicuous.

The two robbers had Chastity up against an abandoned car. "Take off your tights and show us what you're working with," the stocky one of the two demanded.

"Please don't rape me," Chastity pleaded, crying now because she was scared that they were going to kill her.

He pointed the gun at her head. "You have 10 seconds to drop your tights or you die now."

They were going to kill her anyway, so it didn't matter if they had fun or not. They just wanted some of her light-skin pussy after seeing how phat she was.

As Chastity gripped her tights, and pulling them down, everything happened in slow motion.

"Boc, boc" was the only sound heard, before two more shots: "Boc, boc."

Both men fell to the ground, leaking blood all over the place. Chastity looked up and saw a brown-skinned, skinny girl holding the smoking gun.

"Come on, we have to bounce before somebody calls the pigs," she said, grabbing the bag with the money in it, and pulling Chastity out of the lot.

They hopped into the girl's car, leaving Chastity's car there as they peeled off.

"Where do you live?' she asked.

Chastity was still in shock at what just transpired. She looked over at the girl, "Huh?"

"I said, where do you live?"

"40th and Baring," Chastity replied.

"I'll drop you off there, but get somebody to go pick up your car for you. Don't worry you'll be okay. They can't hurt you anymore."

When they pulled up in front of Chastity's apartment, she looked over to the girl. "Thank you for saving my life."

She reached in her book bag and pulled out a knot of money, passing it to the girl.

"That's okay; I don't want your money. Just be careful the next time. Never carry that kind of money around without an escort... or a piece of your own. There are a lot of stick-up kids out there preying on people like you. Make sure you get somebody to pick up your car for you," the girl said.

Chastity hopped out of the car and grabbed her book bag. She shut the door and started walking towards the apartment. She turned around before the girl pulled off.

"Hey!"

The girl rolled down her window. "What's up?" she said, looking at Chastity.

"What's your name?'

The girl smiled before answering, "Erica." She pulled off and turned the corner, leaving Chastity standing there.

TWENTY-ONE

THE INCIDENT THE PREVIOUS night caused Chastity to reconsider the way she moved. She admitted to herself that she was irresponsible by carrying that amount of money by herself, and without protection or someone watching her back.

She knew how to shoot and was very good at it, because every time she went down to Florida, E.J. would take her to the firing range. She just chose not to carry a weapon.

All that had changed now, because she was at the gun store on 69th Street purchasing a 9mm Beretta. They ran her background check though NCIC on the spot, instead of making her wait a couple of days.

She walked out with her brand-new toy on her hip and two extra, fully loaded clips in her purse. That night made her become unbreakable, and if you pulled a gun on her, you better use it. She never killed anyone before, but she would to save her own life. When she got into her car, her cell phone rang. She grabbed it out of her purse and answered it.

"Hey baby, how are you doing?" she asked, already knowing who was calling.

"Don't you 'hey baby' me, why didn't you call me last night and tell me that someone tried to rob you? I had to hear it through a third party. What the fuck is wrong with you?" E.J. replied angrily.

"I was gonna call you but I fell asleep when I got home. I'm okay though, so don't worry."

"Well, I am, so pack your shit. The jet will be on the tarmac waiting for you in two hours."

"I'm not just gonna up and leave everything behind because someone tried to rob me. That's a part of the game, E.J. I got caught slippin'"

"Will you stop being so obstinate and listen for a change? I should have never let you get involved in this business in the first place. I can give you anything and everything you want."

"See, that's just it! I don't want anybody giving me shit. I want to do for myself. You knew that when we first met, so don't act like that now," Chastity said irritated.

"Fine, have it your way. When you're ready to comply, I'm only a phone call away," E.J. said, feeling defeated.

Chastity hung up and threw the phone on the seat. She was tired of people thinking that she was still a little girl. It was time to show everybody that behind her beautiful face and flawless body was as malicious, juggernaut of a person waiting to be unleashed. She pulled off heading for her destination.

* * *

"Damn nigga, what the fuck went wrong? You were supposed to be the one to handle that shit. Who was those lil' niggas anyway?" Reese questioned.

"They were two of the best stick-up kids in Philly. I don't know how they ended up getting bodied. She must have had someone watching her back," Marv replied.

Reese was fuming at the thought of all the money he just squandered on the chance to come up on. He knew he might not get that kind of chance again, because now she would move cautiously and with a team. An idea popped up in his head.

"I need to become the one that she trusts to watch her back. If I can get close to her, it will be easier for me to get the drop on her," Reese said.

"How will you do that?"

"She told me that she needed me to be her muscle, so that's exactly what I'm gonna be. When the time is right, I'm gonna take everything from her, even if I have to kill her and her little friend."

"I feel you. Just let me know what you need me to do," Marv said, puffing on the dutch.

"I'll let you know, but if you ever slip up again, you're cut. I don't need that type of distraction around me," Reese said, heading out the door.

Once he sped off in his wheels, he began formulating a plan that would get him where he needed to be. Nobody except Marv knew about his involvement, so he was in the clear for now. Just to make sure, he was headed to see the one person that he knew he could gather info from.

* * *

E.J. had just returned home from a long day at the club. He poured himself a glass of orange juice before heading upstairs to his room. When he stepped inside his bedroom and hit the light switch, to his surprise, Chastity was laying on his bed with a thong and nothing else on. She was watching *Famous in 12* on TV. E.J. stood there in shock because the last time he talked to her, they were angry.

"What are you doing here?" he asked, kicking off his shoes as he sat on the bed.

Chastity sat up and looked at him. "I've had a lot of time to think about what you said. I'm really starting to care about you and I can't see myself without you, so I came to apologize for acting like that. Will you forgive me?"

"Only if you forgive me for acting like a fool. I'm glad that you want to live independently. I just want you to be able to call on me whenever you're in trouble," E.J. said, taking off his gun and placing it on the closet.

He went back over to the bed, and Chastity grabbed his belt while unbuckling his pants. She reached inside his boxers and pulled out his dick, placing it inside of her mouth. She moaned, sucked, and slurped on it, as it drove E.J. crazy. He grabbed her head and started fucking her mouth like it was her hot pussy.

"Wow baby, I should make you mad more often," he said, watching as his dick went in and out of her mouth.

He started playing with her breasts, squeezing her erect nipples with his fingers. E.J. couldn't do anything but close his eyes, while Chastity's tongue made circles around the tip of his fully hard penis. She grabbed his balls and started massaging them, as she continued to work her mouth like a pro.

"It's my turn to satisfy you now, baby girl," E.J. said, as he slid his hand down to her thong.

He pulled them off, revealing her swollen pussy lips that were already soaked and wet. He began to slowly rub her clitoris, causing a soft seductive moan to escape her mouth.

"Oh baby, I can't take it any longer. I want to feel your tongue on my pussy now," Chastity replied.

Chastity slowly scooted back a little so that E.J. could get on the bed. She spread her legs in anticipation of what was about to take place. E.J. took the rest of his clothes off before lying in between Chastity's thighs.

He licked and slowly started to tongue-kiss her clit. The way his tongue moved around her love muscles made her nut in his mouth within the first three minutes. E.J. lifted his head smiling, as her juices dripped down his chin. He then went back down and continued to give her orgasm after orgasm.

Chastity opened her legs even wider, grabbing his head and pushing his face deeper into her pussy. He took two fingers and stuck them in her ass. He fingered her ass while he ate her out, causing her to explode extra hard from the double penetration.

"Ohhhh, shitttt," she screamed out in total bliss. Her whole body shook in pure delight.

E.J. wasn't finished with her just yet. He leaned up and lay on top of her, kissing her passionately. The whole time she was rubbing on his dick, trying to make him enter her love hole.

E.J. stopped kissing her and stopped to look at how beautiful she was. Her beauty would intimidate any female out there. She could be with any man in the world, but she was here with him. He said he would never let her go again.

When he entered her, Chastity let out a soft moan that turned E.J. on even more. Nothing had ever felt so good to Chastity, as he was stroking her insides passionately and caressing her body. For the next few minutes, there was only erratic breathing and the sounds of E.J.'s body slapping against Chastity's pelvis.

Chastity was matching every stroke with her own. She was literally throwing the pussy back at him.

"Yes, baby, take your pussy. It's all yours," she said through heavy breathing.

They both reached climax in unison. Afterwards, they laid in the bed exhausted from the powerful sexcapade that they just indulged in. E.J. played with her hair, as she laid on his chest.

"Baby girl, I'm in a position to make sure that your every dream can and will come true. All of your wants and desires will be fulfilled. All you have to do is stay here with me. I know you like doing things yourself, and believe me, I respect that. I'm in love with you; and if you don't want to stay, I'll still be in love with you," E.J. said, holding her tight.

Chastity was at a loss for words. She couldn't understand how he just wanted her to up and leave the business that she was successfully running.

"Let me at least have a few months to think about it, please. I will let you know by then."

"Take your time, baby. I'll wait forever for you."

They lay there together and fell asleep in each other's arms. All that was on Chastity's mind was getting back to the "City of Brotherly Love" in a couple days to get back to the money. She had a surprise for niggas this time. If they crossed her, they would have hell to pay. That went for anybody who got in her way of keeping the lifestyle that she had grown so accustomed to living.

TWENTY-TWO

CHASTITY PULLED HER BRAND new Jaguar F-type, R-coupe up to the Spaghetti House on Washington Avenue. It had been a month since the incident had occurred, and life was obviously good. Her product was in high demand all over the tristate area, and she was making more money than she could count. At first, people didn't like the fact that she was a female taking over a predominantly male organization, but after a while, everyone began embracing her savvy ways.

People all around town started realizing that she wasn't a typical young beauty. She was a woman on a mission. She was about to have a meeting with some niggas that came through from Altoona, Pennsylvania. Chastity heard that it was a lot of money out there to be made, and she couldn't pass up the chance to really capitalize off of it.

She walked in the Spaghetti House, turning the attention of every nigga that was sitting down towards her. Even the females couldn't help but stare out of envy, jealousy, or just lust at what passed before their eyes. Everything about her demanded attention, and she always got it. When she saw who she was looking for, she walked over and sat at the table opposite them.

"I'm glad you finally decided to join my team. The transition from the old product to the new should go rather smooth. Once everyone out there tries Numbers, there will be no turning back. Now, what kind of work can you handle right now?" Chastity asked Rob and Boo.

"We need to talk about some numbers first. After that, we can discuss how much we want," Boo said, not feeling the fact that a woman was trying to negotiate a deal for them.

Sensing the way that he was uncomfortable with dealing with a woman, Chastity decided to make him a believer.

"Well, since you're not ready to tell me how much you need, then I guess this meeting is over."

She got up from the table and headed for the door when Rob stopped her. "Wait, Chastity! Come back and talk for a minute."

She didn't need their business, because truth be told, she could have easily just sent a squad of niggas out there to take over the streets. She was trying not to be selfish, plus they knew the area better than her people did. She sat back down at the table and began grilling Boo.

"So, how much are you willing to cop from me? Then I'll give you a price."

"We can move a lot of work out there, more than you think we can. If it's not a problem, I'm trying to cop around 3,000 bundles," Rich said.

"If you want that many then you might as well grab a whole key. My question to you is, can you move that much work at a rapid pace?" Chastity asked.

Rob was feeling unsure of himself, but he didn't want to turn down an offer as sweet as this one. "I'll take it, and yes my crew can handle that quantity and any other quantity of work that you can distribute. When can we pick it up? Because I don't want to go back empty-handed."

"As long as you have the money, we can send you on your way today. The price is $80,000, but I'm willing to give it to you for $70,000. Is that price up your alley?"

"That price is perfect. I have the money in the car right now, so do whatever it is you need to do to get the product here," Boo said, testing her to see if she really had some pull.

Chastity dialed something into her phone, and then it beeped, letting her know she had a response. She smiled at the message while typing something else, before putting her phone down.

"Let's go to your ride and see the cash," she said, placing a hundred on the table for the waitress.

They walked outside to Rob and Boo's car. Rob opened up the trunk and grabbed the briefcase that sat under the spare tire. Chastity watched how carelessly they moved. If they were pulled over in that car with all that work, they would be done for life.

"Here is the $20,000 right here." Rob said, taking 10 grand off the top.

"Why are you taking money out of there?"

"It's eighty grand in here, but now it's only seventy, see," he said, showing her. "You can count it yourself if you want."

"I will," Chastity said, signaling two guys sitting in a car across the street.

Rob and Boo never even noticed the two niggas watching the whole scene. They thought that she was there on her own. It's a good thing that they weren't trying to be deceptive, or they would be dead.

One of the guys came across the street and grabbed the briefcase from Rob so that he could count it in the car. They had a money counter in there for times like this. After counting the money, he gave Chastity a head nod, letting her know it was all there.

"Here you go, boys," she said, throwing them a set of keys. "That is to that Cadillac SRX right there. Since y'all will be working with me, I can't let you get caught slippin' like you would be if you drive the work back in your own car. The Cadillac has a stash box in it, so you can keep everything in there. When you come out here again, I expect you to be in it. The instructions are on the seat. Read them and throw them away!"

"Thank you," Boo said, loosening up.

"No problem. Hit me up when you need to re-up," she said, jumping into her Jaguar.

She pressed the button to start the car and Jeezy's *Biggest Movie Ever* came out of the sound system. Rob and Boo watched as she cruised down the street bopping her head.

"I got some niggas out of town, that's cashing out whatever. I got some bitches on my team; that will take shit wherever. . ."

* * *

Kita had just left from seeing a couple of workers on 22nd and Wharten and was heading for her crib. She wanted to drop off the money before she headed to the other trap houses, when she pulled up to a stop sign, and a car hit her rear bumper.

She had just bought the Range Rover GT, so it pissed her off that someone hit her shit. She pulled over to the side of the curb and stepped out of the car.

The driver of the other vehicle also stepped out. He walked up to Kita and looked at the damage.

"I see it's only a little fender bender. How much do I owe you?" he asked.

"Well for starters, you can give me your insurance information and I'll contact my insurance company."

"Do you have a pen?" he said, pretending to search for one.

She walked back towards her door; and as she reached inside to grab her purse, she felt something push into her back.

"If you scream, you die. All I want is the money and nothing will even happen to you."

Kita stood there silently, but knew that she better comply or else she would be shot. Thinking that it was some random robbery, she passed him the money out of her purse.

"No sweetie, I'm talking about that book bag on the floor right there," he said.

"Fuck man!" Kita replied, passing him the bag.

"Now pass me those keys, and I'll be on my way."

After giving him the truck keys, he ran back to his car and jumped in, leaving her standing there angry as hell.

"Nigga, you better hope that I never see you again," she said to herself. He had the audacity to rob her with no mask. One thing about Kita was that she never forgot a face. He robbed her, but he was still cute, she thought, as she got the spare key from the secret compartment under the car. She hopped in and peeled off.

* * *

Reese met Marv at his crib on Ringgold Street. They were sitting in the kitchen counting money.

"This is all the money that she had? Fuck man, I thought she would be carrying way more money than this," Marv said, putting the stacks of money back in the book bag.

"Well now, they are minus $5,800. That's $2,900 a piece for us. Just keep your half out of the bag, and I'll take the bag with me," Reese said.

He was supposed to go with Marv today so that they could handle something with Chastity, but he stayed back planning to rob Kita. He had fucked Kita a couple of times, while he was fucking Rudy, but it was only for the money with her. Now that she was getting gwap, she didn't even look his way, which made his decision to rob her easy. If he would have gone with Mal, he could have hit the jackpot by getting Chastity.

"Who we're getting next?" Marv asked.

"They are going to be on point right now, so if I'm escorting one of them by myself, I will call you. You can rob both of us and we'll split the money when we meet up. I'm out of here now, so go enjoy your money. It's getting dark

169

now, so I'm going to the crib and fuck one of these bitches that keeps calling me.

"Well, just hit me up when the time is right."

* * *

Chastity was lying in bed, talking to E.J. on the phone about what had happened to Kita that day.

"Ever since you added people to your circle, shit has been happening. I'm not going to tell you how to run your shit, but you need to reconsider whom you keep close. Not everybody is your friend. I had to learn that the hard way," E.J. told her.

"Yeah, you're right, and I'll start thinking more precisely before I move now. I'll talk to you tomorrow. I love you," she said, ending the call.

She got up and went into the room with Rudy. She sat on the bed, watching Rudy looking at her account on her tablet.

"We are killing the game right now, Chas. If my balance looks like this, I can only imagine what yours looks like."

Chastity just smiled at her friend, because she said the same thing when she checked hers a half hour earlier.

"All this money doesn't mean anything if we get caught slippin'. From now on, move discretely so that nobody knows what's going on. Kita could have been hurt if she didn't give up the cash. If it ain't one of us collecting money with a stash car, then it better be Kita, Neatra, or Sharon. I have five new top-of-the-line stash cars coming in tomorrow. We're going to junk the other ones and use these," Chastity said.

"Okay, what about the new shipment that we're expecting from Florida tomorrow? If we don't have the vehicles to pick it up, we can't get it."

"Don't worry about that. They will be arriving on schedule along with the cars," Chastity replied, winking her eyes.

"Girl, you are one sneaky bitch," she said, already knowing what she meant by that.

They both started laughing at Rudy's remark. "Seriously, though, it's time to roll out of this apartment. I've talked to Nyia and she has a 4-bedroom, 2.5-bath house for us to look at in the morning," Chastity said.

"Where at?"

"Out in Wynfield near Cityline Avenue. It's beautiful out that way, so I can't wait to see what the house looks like."

"Well, shit, let's get some sleep, because I'm anxious, too. You know I don't like getting up early, but I will for that."

"I'll see you in the morning, bitch," Chastity said, exiting the room.

She went back in her room and lay on her bed. She thought about how far she had come from being molested by her uncle to being put out on the street with nothing. Now she had money for days, a rich boyfriend, her own apartment, and her soon-to-be own house. Life was good for her right now. But there was still one thing that she needed to do to be free from pain, and that was to get even with her uncle. She didn't want to kill him. She just wanted to make him hurt a little for what he put her through. As soon as she thought of a plan, then, and only then, would she carry it out.

TWENTY-THREE

HAKEEM SAT IN HIS cell reading a letter from one of his jump-offs. He heard from a couple of new dudes that just came though that some chick was running shit out there. They called her the Queen of the Streets. Now the letter he was reading had just confirmed it. Chastity and her crew had shit on smash.

Hakeem felt like a fool for turning his back on her. He never would have imagined that she would be in that type of position. If he could only get out of here, he would be able to try to control his blocks again.

He was now in Gratersford State Institute. The classification team had classified him there because he put in for a hardship so that they wouldn't ship him across state. As he sat on his bunk, he wondered what kind of dirt he could dig up on Chastity. He decided to get his jump-off to tell him everything she could about her.

"Count is clear, count is clear," the lady said over the intercom. Hakeem ran over to the phone once the doors opened. He called Jovon, and as soon as she accepted his call, he put his plan in motion.

When his time was up on the phone, he chilled on the block waiting to walk over to the chow hall to eat dinner.

"Yo, Keem, what's up with you?" one of the inmates asked him.

"Shit, I'm chillin' man, just waiting to get that bar-b-cue chicken tonight, so I can put in my chi-chi," Hakeem told the dude.

"Is you going out to night yard, because we have a football game against B-block?"

"Yeah, I guess I am. My lil' chick just told me she wasn't coming up tonight. I ain't sweating it though. I'll be ready. What time do we play?"

"We're the first game. So after dinner, gear up," the dude said, heading back to this cell. Hakeem went back to his cell and pulled out his picture tickets and his popcorn ticket.

After the game, he was gonna grab some popcorn for the movie that night, and then he was going to take yard flicks to send to a couple of bitches. He had been working out every day, so he wanted to show his bitches what they were missing.

"C-block, chow time! Report to the cafeteria. This is your first call," they announced on the PA system.

Hakeem and the other inmates headed to grab their food. He couldn't wait to make the phone call that would change his current status and hopefully get him out of here.

* * *

On Friday night, Chastity and Rudy were getting ready so that they could hit up the club scene. After about 15 minutes of debating, they decided to go to 8th Street Lounge, on 8th and Callowhill. They hadn't been to that club in a while since Ziaire's had been their spot.

"You ready, Rudy? We still have to pick up Sharon," Chastity said, putting on some Rogue (by Rihanna) perfume.

"Yeah, I'll be down in a minute. I just have to put my stilettos on and some of this new perfume. Why haven't you used any of that Pulse (by Beyoncé) perfume yet that's on your dress?"

"Because you're always using it," Chastity said smiling.

They both grabbed their jackets and headed for the door. After setting the alarm, they hopped in the Navigator limo that was parked outside waiting for them. Ever since their first time they used the limo service, they called them every time they wanted to go out.

Chastity was rocking the shit out the white Juan Carlos Obando dress, while Rudy looked scandalous in an extra tight-fitted Yuki dress. It was so short, that it left nothing to the imagination.

"I can't wait to get to the club. I want to see how many niggas this dress pulls me tonight," Rudy said.

"Keep fucking around and your freaky-ass is gonna catch something. That's if you ain't already caught it."

Rudy put her middle finger up at Chastity, as the two shared a laugh.

"On some real shit though, you and E.J. need to make up, because y'all were made for each other," Rudy said seriously.

When Chastity had surprised E.J. by going to see him, everything was okay. The next day though, being suspicious, she looked through his dresser and came across a photo of him and a female with a beautiful caramel complexion. She asked him about her, but he wouldn't give her the answer that she was looking for. She ended up leaving that morning instead of staying for the rest of the time.

"Don't mess my night up, I'm trying to go out and enjoy myself. All that boyfriend drama we can save for another day. Pass me a glass of Moscato so I can get a little buzz before we get there," Chastity said, checking herself in the mirror inside the limo.

* * *

8th Street Lounge was jumping and people were lined up all the way down to 9th Street. Women had barely any clothes on, and the niggas were flossing with iced-out watches and chains.

A red Ferrari 599 GTO, with 21-inch Techart Formula IV sports wheels, pulled up in front of the club, followed by three all-black Porsche Cayenne trucks. The driver of the

Ferrari stepped out in an all-red Versace suit, causing the ladies in line waiting to get in lust. He knew he would have that effect on them, as he stood there waiting for his henchmen to exit their vehicles.

Nasty and his crew made their way to the two bouncers standing by the door. The bouncers greeted him and his crew, letting them inside without even checking them. All the ladies were trying to get their attention, but they just brushed them off and kept it moving.

Nasty, whose real name was Maurice Turner, was one of the most notorious drug kingpins in New York. He moved on the outskirts of Philly so that he could keep a low profile from the feds a year ago. Since being out here, he expanded his organization throughout all areas of Philly. Nasty sold cocaine, and it quickly boosted his status, making him the primary source for the product.

They called him Nasty for two reasons. First, he grew up overweight, always eating fattening food. At age 14, he weighed a little over 300 pounds. Kids used to make fun of him and teased him in school. Now at age 20, he still weighed 300 pounds, but it was all muscle. No one ever tried to make fun of him now. If someone got on his wrong side, they'd end up in a ditch somewhere. He was now well respected by everyone.

The second reason was that he was very open in the bedroom with the ladies. He would do anything except let someone play in his anal region. That was the only thing that was off limits to him.

When they entered the club, they headed straight to the VIP section. 2 Chains was blaring through the speakers, as the ladies and niggas partied on the dance floor.

"This shit is jumping up in here. Look at all those bad bitches right there," Nasty's right-hand-man said.

Nasty smirked as he summoned the waitress over to him. She walked over wearing boy shorts and a sports bra.

"What can I get for you tonight?" she asked.

Nasty pulled out two rubber bands of hundred dollar bills and started peeling off about 50 of them.

"Let me get bottles of Cîroc and Ace of Spades for everyone in VIP. If you need more money, just come back and holla at me," he replied, placing the money on the tray she was carrying. He then peeled off another $100 and stuck it in her bra. "That right there is your first tip of the night. Treat us good, and there will be more where that came from."

"Don't I take care of your every time you come here?" she said flirtatiously.

Nasty smacked her on the ass, as she went to get the bottles for him and his crew.

They were enjoying their night when he noticed the most beautiful lady that he had ever witnessed walk into the club with her bad friends. She had a body that would put Kim Kardashian, J-Lo, and Beyoncé to shame. From the look of their attire, you could tell they were all about money. He stared at the females until they sat in one of the VIP booths next to his.

"What is this, some kind of special occasion tonight? Because this place is filled to capacity," Sharon said, as they signaled for the waitress.

"I don't know, but it is jumping in here," Chastity responded.

The waitress walked up and they placed their orders. She scurried off to retrieve their drinks.

"I'm about to hit the dance floor. Y'all coming, or are you gonna sit up here and act all conceited?" Rudy commented, headed for the dance floor.

"Let's get it," Chastity responded, as she and Sharon headed to the floor behind Rudy.

Wale & Juicy J's *Clappers* filled the speakers, making all the girls in the club go crazy. Soon as they said, *"Showty got a big ol' butt,"* Chastity started popping her ass. Niggas were trying to get in back of her, but she brushed them off, as she and her girls started grinding on each other and having a ball.

Kita walked into the club late and then joined her sisters out on the dance floor. After dancing to a couple of songs, they went back up to the VIP booth to chill.

"Where the fuck is our drinks at?" Rudy said.

"Here she comes now," Sharon said, watching the waitress pass each girl a glass.

"What is this?" Chastity asked, looking at the drink the waitress passed her.

"That's compliments of the guy sitting over there. It's called *Tap that Ass*," she said.

"What's in it?" she said, tasting it. "It tastes good."

"It's a combination of Hennessy, red and yellow Alizé, a splash of cranberry juice and topped off with soda water. I tried it before, and it's good. Will that be all?' the waitress asked.

"We're fine, thank you. Who the fuck is that though?" Rudy asked.

"I don't know. But from the way he's throwing money around, he must be getting it," Sharon replied.

"Well, we about to show him how some ballin' chicks from the PJ's get down," Chastity said, walking off towards the bar.

"What is that girl up to now? She always got a trick up her sleeve," Kita said, tasting her drink.

They were enjoying the music, when Chastity came back with stacks and stacks of dollar bills. She placed them on the table while gulping down the rest of her drink.

"Come on girls, let's make it rain in this bitch."

Everybody grabbed a stack of bills and stood near the rail of the VIP section. They started tossing money in the air without a care in the world. People on the dance floor tried desperately to snatch money out of the air. The DJ switched the song, and Jim Jones' *Ballin'* blared through the speakers.

Nasty and his crew just sat there and observed these women putting on a show for the crowd. He watched the way she moved her hips, and he could only imagine what she would be like in bed. He decided to try his hand and see where it got him.

He walked over to her and whispered in her ear, "Can I get a minute of your time, ma?"

"That's all you got, 'cause as you can see, I'm chillin' with my girls," Chastity responded nonchalantly.

"Well, I've been watching you all night, and I would like to get to know you better. Did you enjoy the drink I sent you?"

"It was interesting."

"Well, I'm trying to get up out of there and do just that. Are you rolling with me?" he asked directly to the point.

Chastity admired his straight to the pointedness, but he was too cocky with it.

"Damn, what kind of girl you think I am? Do your homework on me before you approach me like that again."

Nasty, trying to keep face, said, "No disrespect, ma. I just thought. . ."

"You didn't think," she said, cutting him off. "I'm gonna pass through. Come on y'all, let's hit the floor again."

She and the girls slid back out to the floor, and started dropping low and winding to the music.

* * *

After enjoying themselves for a few hours, Chastity was ready to leave. She had too much to drink, which caused her to be tipsy. As they were headed for the door, Kita noticed a familiar face also exiting the club. She looked closely and instantly remembered who it was.

"That's the nigga right there that rob me. I'll never forget that pussy face," Kita said.

Chastity, Rudy, and Sharon looked to see whom she was talking about. They all walked and went straight over to him and some bitch. Chastity wasn't into this type of drama, but she was ready to throw down if she had to.

Marv was grabbing on the thick girl's ass, while they were walking towards his car.

"Yo," Chastity said, trying to get his attention. "Yo nigga, you hear me calling you?"

Marv stopped and turned around thinking he was busted by this girl. When he saw who it was, he smiled, thinking, *what these bitches want?*

"Nigga, you took something from me, and I want it back," Chastity stated.

"I don't know what the fuck you're talking about, so take that shit to somebody else," Marv responded.

"Oh, so now you don't know what she talking about, huh? You robbed me at gunpoint, nigga. Do you remember now?" Kita said, stepping towards him.

He instantly remembered her, but he played it off. He was mad that he didn't rock her ass to sleep (kill her), when he robbed her 'cause he thought she was gonna go to the cops. But since she didn't, he knew she was a hood bitch.

"Give me my shit back, and we won't have a problem. I want every last dollar, and I want it now," Chastity said with authority.

"What these bitches talking about?" one of Marv's boys walked up and asked.

"Who you calling a bitch, you pussy," Rudy shot back.

"Just give me my shit and you can leave," Chastity said.

Marv looked around, and with one quick motion smacked the shit out of Chastity, causing her to stumble backwards.

"Watch who the fuck you talking to, bitch," he said firmly.

Rudy and her sisters were about to attack, when his boy pulled out his gun aiming at them, waiting for someone to pop fly.

"Matter of fact, I seen all that money you were throwing around in the club, so you might as well let me take that off your hands," Marv replied.

Chastity was still a little distraught from the smack, as she was holding her face.

Nasty and a few of his goons were standing outside, picking which chicks they were going to take to the motel that night, when he saw the dude smack Chastity. He continued to watch, thinking it was her boyfriend lashing out for coming out of the house like that. When he saw him back out on her (pull a gun), his street instincts kicked in.

"Yo strap up," he yelled to his boys, as he pulled out his 40 cal and walked towards Chastity.

"I'm not giving you shit. Do what you gotta do, but you will get yours," Chastity responded, refusing to back down.

"This bitch is a feisty one," Marv said, pointing the gun at her chest, readying to lay her down.

Chastity was scared shitless, but she wouldn't show this clown one ounce of fear.

Just as he was about to pull the trigger, two shots hit him dead in the chest, knocking him down. His boy tried to aim his gun, but was too slow. "Boc, boc, boc."

The shots entered his body, killing him before he hit the ground. Nasty walked up to Marv's body and was about to finish the job, when Chastity stopped him.

She took the gun from him and emptied the clip into his body. Rudy, Sharon, Kita, and even Nasty and his goons watched in amazement. The gun's chamber clicked back, letting her know that it was empty, so she dropped it on the ground.

People began scattering in every direction at the sound of the gunfire. Nasty snatched the gun off the ground and grabbed Chastity's arm.

"Come on, ma, we have to get out of here before the pigs pull up," he said, pulling her towards his car.

"Get these girls out of here now," he commanded.

Nasty and Chastity jumped in his Ferrari and sped off, while his boys and her girls jumped in the Porsche trucks.

They drove in silence for a few minutes, before either of them said a word.

"Are you okay?" Nasty asked her.

She continued to stare out the window in a trance. She had just killed somebody, and it wasn't sitting well on her conscious... or her stomach.

"Pull over please," she said, not even turning to look at him.

"I have to get you out of here before we both get booked," Nasty countered.

"Please pull over now. I have to throw up," she responded, with her voice growing louder.

Nasty pulled over to the side of the road. Chastity opened the door and leaned out, letting everything she ate that day out. After she finished puking, she shut the car door. Nasty gave her a brand new shirt he had in a bag on the floor.

"You can wipe your face with this."

"Thank you," she said, looking out the window as they rode over the Ben Franklin Bridge. "Where are we going?"

"I have a crib over in Paulsboro that I never use. We are going to hide out there until we find out what the streets are saying. Don't worry; there won't be nothing to link us to the scene of the crime."

They pulled up to a mini mansion that was surrounded by an electronic fence. Nasty hit a button on his keychain, and the gate began sliding open. He pulled through, closing it behind him, and then drove into a garage.

Chastity noticed the line of luxury cars and was impressed. It was nothing like what E.J. had, but it definitely gave him a run for his money. He had two different-colored Maseratis, an Aston Martin, and a Bentley Mulsanne.

"Come on in," he said, as they stepped out of the Ferrari.

When they entered the house, Chastity noticed how spectacular the inside was; it was huge and it was surprisingly clean for a man's house.

"I'll show you around real quick," he stated, leading her through each room.

He had Travertine stone floors, Brazilian hardwood cabinets, imported Parisian furniture, and a host of other shit. She was shocked at how this stranger was living.

"Why did you help me?" she asked, realizing that she was involved in a murder with someone she didn't even know.

"I don't respect niggas that put their hands on females. My mother was beaten when I was young, so I killed the nigga," he said, not caring that he confessed to her. "Excuse my ignorance, I'm Nasty. What's your name?"

"My name is Chastity. Why do they call you Nasty?" she questioned.

Nasty smiled at her question, and then answered, "I'll tell you another time. This is definitely not the right moment to be explaining that."

She smiled herself at that answer. "I guess you're right. So Nasty, what do you do?"

"I'm in the pharmaceutical business," he replied. "What about you and what was that all about?"

"That nigga robbed one of my workers a week ago, so he deserved everything that he got tonight," she said, as they sat on the plush sofa. "I'm also in the pharmaceutical business. Maybe you heard of my product... Numbers?"

Chastity was giving up too much information to a guy who she met only a couple of hours ago. By the time she realized that, it was too late to take it back. She hoped that he didn't have any treachery in his blood.

"So, you're the infamous Queen of the Streets. You have the heroin game on smash. Well, I'm the King of the Streets out here. I have the coke on smash. It's really nice to finally meet you. King and Queen of the Streets, we could make a great team," he said smiling.

She smiled, "Sorry I already have a team, but we can definitely do something together."

Nasty's dick grew rock hard at the way she said that. He had been staring at her ass all night, and now he had her in his presence all to himself. She picked up on what he was thinking.

"No, I'm not that easy, Boo. I was talking about business-wise. We can do business together if you're interested. I can supply you, and you can supply me," she said, killing his hopes for the night.

They talked damn near until the sun came up, each realizing that they had a lot in common. The physical attraction wasn't there yet for Chastity; but mentally, he had left a lasting impression on her. He showed her to one of the rooms so she could get some sleep. After calling her friends, and making sure they were straight, she took off her dress and lay in the bed in just her panties and bra. She dozed right off as soon as her head hit the pillow.

TWENTY-FOUR

"WE HAVE BREAKING NEWS from the shootout that took place outside of a night club this morning. Police say that two men were gunned down right outside of 8th Street Lounge at 2:20 this morning. Witnesses say that Marvin Wright and an accomplice were fatally shot by an unknown male, while trying to rob a female who was leaving the club.

Marvin Wright was wanted for a number of robberies around the west and north Philly suburbs. His brother is doing 20 years at Gratersford for a gun and drug charge. His accomplice's name was Saleen Parker. Both men had I.D. on them. This is just the 15th homicide this year. We'll have more on this case as it unfolds. I'm Melissa Maghee reporting for Eyewitness News," the news reporter said, as Hakeem watched in horror.

Marvin was his little brother. He was only 17 years old, and his birthday was the following week. Hakeem knew what Marv was out there doing, because he was the one who showed him about that life. He just couldn't believe that the streets finally got him.

He started thinking about the letter that he sent him two days earlier. Marv had told him that he was working for Reese, doing lil' jobs here and there. Hakeem had written him back that night telling him not to trust Reese because he was a snake. Now that he heard about his, he knew whatever Reese had him doing; it got his little brother bodied, along with his friend who was only 15 years old.

That reason alone made Hakeem's decision to do the unthinkable that much easier. He needed to get out of jail, so he decided to give up his ex in order to do so. He didn't live by the code of the streets anymore. He lost all his morals and dignity when his brother died. Fuck the saying, "If you can't do the time, don't do the crime." It was get-back time; and whatever it took for him to get out, that's what he was going to do.

He sat in his cell and wrote a letter to the DEA, informing them that he needed to talk to them ASAP. He had no shame in what he was about to do. After he finished writing the letter, he placed it in an envelope and sealed it. He addressed it, walked out of the cell, and put it in the mailbox.

"Yo, Keem, are you ordering from the Lifer's Commissary this month?" his boy Meech asked him.

"Yeah, do you have an extra slip?"

"I put it on your bunk for you. Make sure you fill it out by the end of the day. They are gonna pick them up after dinner."

"Cool," Hakeem said, as he grabbed some ice from the ice machine before heading back to his cell.

He lay on his bunk and watched the rest of the news, the whole time thinking how he would get his revenge on everybody that crossed him. He just hoped that his plan would work. He had the whole weekend to formulate a plan so that the DEA agents would buy his story.

* * *

Chastity had just finished watching the news when she realized the extent of what had happened the night before. She was lucky that no one had recognized her at the club. So far, she was in the clear.

She stepped out of bed and peeked out the door, looking for Nasty. When she didn't see him, she eased down the hall to the bathroom. She didn't feel like putting her dress on to take a piss, so she went in her thong and bra. After taking a piss, she was returned back to the room when Nasty came out carrying breakfast.

"Sorry, I didn't know you were here, and I couldn't find anything to throw on real quick so that I could take a tinkle," Chastity said smiling.

Nasty couldn't take his eyes off of her perfect body. Her abs and tight physique had him mesmerized monetarily.

"I brought breakfast for us," he said, handing her the platter.

She didn't even try to cover herself up or run in the room. She just opened the lid of the platter.

"Damn, my favorite... pancakes, cheese eggs, turkey bacon, and home fries. Thank you," Chastity said, staring at him.

She didn't want to admit that she really wanted him to sneak in her room last night and eat her pussy. She had woken up that morning horny as hell. A smirk came across her face as she turned around, heading back to her room and throwing a little extra in her walk.

Nasty's dick was poking out from his shorts, as he watched her ass swallow up her thong. He went back in his room, hoping that he didn't get blue balls from being so hard.

As he watched ESPN, Chastity knocked on the door, causing him to look up. She was still only wearing her thong and bra.

"I just wanted to show you my appreciation for saving my life last night. If you weren't there, it would probably have been me and my girls on the news instead of those two pussies," she said, walking up to him, grabbing his crotch, and yanking his dick out of his shorts.

Nasty knew what time it was. He opened his legs as she kneeled down, taking him into her warm mouth. She sucked his dick so good that she literally had him running from her.

Not to be outdone, he decided to show her why they called him Nasty. He stood up and ripped her thong off, bent her over the bed, and got down on his knees. He spread her ass cheeks apart, licking and spitting in her hole.

Without thinking, he began eating her asshole. The feeling of his tongue sent chills down Chastity's spine. She was enjoying the sensation of his tongue inside her ass. Nobody had ever done that to her before, not even E.J. He fucked her in the ass, but never ate it.

He licked every hole on her body, making her cum more than six times. When he finally entered that phat pussy of hers, he came within two minutes because of how good it was. He didn't let that stop him though, he was back hard in a minute, and right back into her wet-wet. He was relentlessly trying to knock her walls out as he pounded away.

By the time they finally finished, Chastity couldn't even close her legs together. Her pussy was so sore that she couldn't sit straight up inside of the car while Nasty drove her home.

When she got home, she filled in Rudy on everything that took place after they separated the night before, and even what she and Nasty did that morning. It shocked her that Chastity actually cheated on E.J., but she really wanted her to get caught doing it. She wouldn't tell her friend to her face, but she wanted to fuck him. Rudy would imagine the two of them fucking every time she masturbated.

"Damn girl, looks like you had a crazy night and an exciting morning to make up for it," Rudy stated.

"I guess you can say that."

"So what are you gonna do about your man in Miami? You gonna have to see him once we run out of work. As a matter of fact, we need to go and check our supply because we might have to see him sooner than we think," Rudy said, hoping that she would be able to take the trip with Chastity the next time.

Chastity wasn't expecting to hear his name. She hadn't talked about him or to him ever since they argued about that picture. He tried calling and texting her, but she wouldn't answer or respond.

"I'm not thinking about him right now. We are about to expand our business to a whole new level. Nasty has the coke business on smash, so we are going to let each other eat on each of our respective areas. With this new expansion, we might have to double our next order. I'm gonna take a quick shower and then we can go check our stash house," Chastity said, stepping out of her dress.

"Look at your freaky ass. Where is your thongs you were wearing? Let me guess, you let him keep them as a souvenir?"

Chastity smiled as she ran upstairs, leaving her dress on the floor. She hollered down the steps, "Wouldn't you like to know, bitch!"

* * *

Two months had passed since Chastity and Nasty had met. They were spending so much time together that she actually forgot about E.J. She had sent the money to him and Pedro without going down there herself because she didn't want to see him.

Pedro started cutting her supply back because E.J. wanted her to call him. Pedro was reluctant to do it at first, but ended up doing it anyway out of respect for his partner and friend. Still, Chastity never called or even complained about the cut in product. She thought it was a problem getting the work over from Mexico.

She and Nasty were in the pizza shop at 21st and Oregon Avenue when Chris walked in to grab Stromboli. He walked to the counter and ordered a soda to go with it. When he turned around to leave, he noticed Chastity sitting on Nasty's lap. She didn't even see him until he got closer and spoke to her.

"What's up, Chastity? Who is this dude?" he asked, as she looked up shocked.

"Uh, hey Chris. What are you doing down here?"

"Don't even worry about it. Enjoy yourself," he replied, as he walked out and jumped in his car.

"Who was that?" Nasty asked suspiciously.

"That was my connect."

"Why was he looking at your all sideways? Y'all was fucking around or something?"

"No, I was messing with his brother. I don't want to talk about it anymore though, so drop it," she said nervously, because she knew that E.J. was going to snap.

* * *

Instead of Hakeem giving up Chastity to the DEA, he gave up Chris, thinking if he goes, that would stop her flow, and she would run back to him once he was home. They had been trying to dig something up on him but couldn't find anything, so they dropped the case, which left Hakeem fuming. He really thought he was about to get home sooner.

Now not only was he stuck in prison, but he also had better hope that no one found out what he had done. They would label him a snitch and probably attempt to kill him.

He called his jump-off, Jovon, to see what the word on the street was, but she hadn't heard anything. She told him that she was trying to get him a lawyer who could work on giving his time back. He informed her that it wouldn't be easy, because he took a plea. She said that she was still going to try for him.

After hanging up the phone, he decided to get a pass and head over to the barbershop.

"Ms. James, can I get a pass for the barbershop?" he asked the female correctional officer at the desk.

"Mr. Wright, it is too late for you to get a pass. You will have to wait until tomorrow," she said, as she continued her conversation with the other correctional officer sitting there.

Hakeem didn't even complain, he just waited for the yard call, so he could go hit the weight pile. He decided to get used to being there for the next 20 years. Maybe he could get out early on parole, but it was a strong possibility that he wouldn't. Either way, he was going to make the best of a bad situation.

TWENTY-FIVE

AFTER TALKING TO CHRIS on the phone, and finding out about Chastity's deception, E.J. called Pedro. His assistant connected the call to an untraceable line so they could talk freely.

"E.J., why are you not here yet? I thought we were gonna watch the baseball game together," Pedro asked.

"Something came up, but I'll still be over there tomorrow for our meeting."

"What's wrong then?"

"I need you to cut all ties with Chastity. She is no longer on our team," E.J. stated.

"What happened? You have to give me more to go on. She is a valuable asset to this business, and she is a good business woman from what I have been seeing so far."

"I need this done, Pedro, because she betrayed me by sleeping with another man."

"Since when have you started going off emotions? Stop wearing your feelings on your chest. You're showing signs of weakness, and I've never seen you do that before. She is responsible for 90% of the heroin in Philly, Jersey, and Delaware, not to mention the other cities that she has added to the organization. What you are asking me to do will affect us all, my friends."

"Trust, me on this Pedro, I know what I'm doing. Chris will run everything the same way. Only thing that's changed as of now is the personnel. Numbers will still do numbers. The name alone is what is making the money. Anybody business-minded can run this operation. I made her, so I want to show her that I can break her."

"Well, this is your decision… and your decision only. It's all on you; and when she calls, I'll tell her I don't know anything. Be careful acting off emotions, they could become your downfall. I'll see you at the meeting tomorrow," Pedro replied, and then ended the call.

E.J. sat on his patio looking out at the beach and sea of water, wondering how it had come to this. He made a risky decision based on jealousy. In his heart, he knew he was wrong, but it was a judgment call that he would have to live with.

* * *

Rudy woke up to the sound of her cell phone ringing. She checked the caller ID and then sent it to voicemail. She lay back down, trying to get some more sleep, when her text alert starting going off. Wanting to see what Chastity kept bugging her about; she got up and dialed her number.

"Why the hell you not answering your phone? I've been calling you all morning. We have a fucking problem," Chastity yelled through the phone.

"What's wrong, Chas? Are you okay?" Rudy asked nervously.

"No, I'm not okay. I tried to contact Pedro today to see when the next shipment would be coming, and he told me it won't!"

"Wait, what do you mean it won't?"

"He said to call E.J. and he will explain. He told me that there won't be any more shipments for me, and that's all he would say. I've been trying to call E.J., but he won't answer."

"Do you think something has happened to him or where it comes from?" Rudy asked.

"I don't know yet, but we are down to the last of our supplies, and we were supposed to have the new shipment two days ago," Chastity answered.

Rudy sat there holding the phone wondering what was happening. They never had this kind of problem before, so neither one of them knew how to respond to it.

"Where are you at now?" Rudy said.

"I'm on my way to see Chris, hoping that he will know what's going on. Tell Nasty that I'll see him later after I take care of business."

"Where is he?"

"In my room probably still asleep."

"Okay, just call me when you find out what the hell is going on. If you need me, I'm only a text or phone call away," Rudy told her.

"Okay, let me try to call him again," she replied, hanging up and dialing E.J.'s number again, Once again, she got his voicemail, so she left another message.

Rudy put on her robe and went to take a shower. She went into Chastity's room to deliver the message to Nasty. When she walked into the room, Nasty was laying in the bed, sleeping butt naked. She looked at his body and then down to his dick. She became instantly wet and she eased back out the door, closing it behind her.

She went to take a shower so she could get dressed and leave to get her hair done.

After taking her shower, she went back to Chastity's room, but this time she knocked on the door.

"Come in," Nasty said.

Rudy opened the door to find him still laying there naked. She turned her head towards the door.

"Chastity said that she'll meet up with you later. She has to take care of something."

"You can turn around, ma. You act like you never seen a naked man before," he said, smoking a dutch.

"I'm good, thank you. But I'm about to leave, so when you do leave, just lock up behind you."

Rudy walked out the door. She wanted to see what he was working with, but she couldn't do that to her friend. "Temptation is a mutha fucka," she said to herself while smiling.

* * *

Chastity pulled up to the car lot at the same time as Chris. When she stepped out of the car, she could tell he wasn't too pleased to see her.

"Chris, can you tell me what's going on with my shipment? It was supposed to be here two days ago," she asked.

"You don't have anything coming. Let that nigga that you been flaunting around here with supply you. Oh my bad, he can't get that pure shit like my brother, can he?"

"Is that what this is all about? Your brother was cheating on me! I saw the pictures in his drawer," she said.

"What pictures did you see?"

"The ones of him and some brown-skin bitch, and some of them with a little boy. Yeah, you're fucking brother has a whole other family," she responded angrily.

"That was his ex-wife. Something went down that I'm not at liberty to discuss with you. You're the one that bit the hand that was feeding you. You made your bed, now go lay in it."

Chastity stood there feeling stupid as Chris walked away from her. He cut her off over another nigga. She didn't think that he would act like that. Determined not to break, she decided to find a new connect. She thought to herself, "How hard could it be?"

She jumped in her wheel and headed for her stash house on Reno Street. She wanted to see if there was enough work there to hold them over for at least the rest of the day.

When she pulled up to the house, her eyes popped wide open, as she looked at the boarded-up crib. Chastity got out of the car and looked around. The whole house had been sealed off.

She saw the owner walking towards her and asked, "What happened here?"

"A couple guys came passed, took everything out, and then boarded up the house. They paid me $20,000 to find somewhere else to live. They even told the four gals to go to the new house and work," the lady said.

Chastity was boiling now, because they took all the money and work that was there. She called Rudy, Sharon, Kita, and Neatra to tell them to check on the other cribs; but just like this one, they ran into the same results. Every crib had been cleaned out and boarded up.

She was furious, so she called E.J.'s phone, but this time he answered on the third ring.

"What the fuck you keep calling my phone for?" he said.

"Why are you doing this to me? I didn't do shit to you," she screamed at him, as tears formed in her eyes.

"You did this to yourself. But don't worry, that New York nigga better head back to where he came from, or he'll be going in a casket. You can take your trifling ass with him too, because you won't be making any money on these streets again unless you sell your ass," he said, and then hung up on her.

Chastity didn't know what to do. He never talked to her that way before. The thought that she could sweet talk him went right out the door. She sat in her car, pondering her next move. She said to herself that she wasn't going to strip anymore. She had plenty of money in her bank account and in the Believe account overseas, so she was good for a while.

Chastity didn't know how to budget money, so she would buy nothing but expensive shit. Everything from her designer clothes to her Victoria Secret panty and bra sets were all top of the line. She was a bad bitch, and she made sure that she lived like one. That's why she decided to tell Nasty that people were going to try and force him out of town.

* * *

"Yo, Hakeem, come see this shit, man. It's about to go down on the news," Meech yelled out of his cell.

Hakeem ran over to the cell to see what had his homey all excited. He stopped in the cell with him.

"What's up, Meech?"

"Hold on! They're about to talk about it right now. Some crazy shit happened today. Here it is now," he said, turning up the volume on the television.

"We're reporting live from Central Station. Just a couple of hours ago, in a surprise drug scandal, two drug lab employees have been arrested in connection with a large amount of drugs disappearing from the Office of the Chief Medical Examiners located in Delaware. In that arrest was John Millson, a forensic investigator, who at one point worked for the Pennsylvania State Police Department. He was laid off because of suspicion of bribing drug dealers for hush money. Pennsylvania and New Jersey have been sending their evidence to this location because of the overwhelming amount of drug testing needing to be done. If it is found that the evidence was tainted, this could be one of the biggest scandals in history, because over 9,700 inmates could be released. A press conference is expected to be held in about 10 minutes. We'll bring that coverage to you live as soon as it's underway. Reporting live from Central State, I'm Melissa Maghee."

"Do you know what the fuck that means, dawg?" Hakeem excitedly asked Meech.

"Do I? It means that we will probably be going home soon. I hope they find something messed up," he stated, turning off the TV.

"Everybody with drug cases right now is hoping for that. If they throw the drugs out, that means the gun is gone, too. I haven't been praying lately, but I'm damn sure going to start now," Hakeem replied.

"I'm gonna be right there on my knees with you on that. This can be the big break that we've been looking for. I'm about to call my girl and tell her to look it up on the internet, and send me a copy of the whole article," Meech stated, hurriedly walking towards the phones.

"I might as well call and do the same thing just in case yours is different from mine."

The smile on their faces, as well as the other inmates' faces, illuminated the block. Everyone felt good about something, even if it was only a slim chance of them getting out on a technicality.

"Count time on your doors," the correctional officer yelled before they could complete their calls.

"Maybe that was a sign right there. I don't think we should say anything until we know for sure that we're bouncing," Meech stated.

Hakeem thought about it as they walked back to their cells for count.

"You're right. I think I'm just gonna slide up outta here and surprise everybody. They will be so shocked that they won't know what to do," Hakeem said.

The whole time he was making that statement, he was thinking about Chastity. She thinks that he won't be home for 20 years, so if he just popped up on her, she might think that he escaped or something. Whatever the case may be, he wanted to get his girl back, and that's what he intended to do.

* * *

"I can't believe that he cut you off like that," Kita said. They were all sitting in the kitchen talking about the drastic chain of events.

"Don't you mean us? If he cut Chastity off, then we all are about to suffer," Neatra said.

"Damn, you're right. And I was just looking for a new crib so that I could move out of these filthy projects," Kita said.

"So what are we gonna do without our hustle? I'm damn sure not going back to no day job. This bitch got me spoiled. Now we can't make no more money right now," Kita said, playfully punching Chastity in the arm.

"Don't worry, I'm working on something. I talked to Nasty and he's going to see if he can find us a nice plug for a while. If he can't, I'll ask him to hook us up with some coke."

"We don't know shit about coke," Rudy said.

"It can't be that hard; besides, Nasty will probably only have us dropping off and picking up. That shit will be easy because we did that shit already," Chastity stated.

"You know he is not gonna let you be in the streets like that anymore. Us on the other hand, we will have to work our asses off to even benefit out of this," Kita admitted.

"We came in this together, so I'm going to grind it out with y'all. I don't care what he says. Y'all my family," Chastity responded.

"That's all it is then. Now can we go find something to eat, because I'm starving?" Sharon said.

"I'll drive," Kita said, as they all headed for her Range Rover.

Chastity felt content around her family. She still felt on top of the world, even though everything was crashing down around her. It reminded her of that song by State Property: *"The sun never shines nit eh ghetto, it only rains in the hood. . ."* She was determined to never get caught up in the storm anymore. She was looking for that sun to shine down on her and her crew.

TWENTY-SIX

A MONTH HAD PASSED and Chastity still couldn't find a reliable connect. Nasty had been looking around, but no one would fuck with him as far as supplying him with heroin. He still had the city on lock with the coke, because it was grade A.

He introduced Chastity to a plug, but the work was garbage. She couldn't even give the shit away. Her money was starting to dwindle, so she found herself relying on Nasty a lot. She wanted to do some work to try and make ends meet until she found a supply that wasn't trash, but Nasty just wanted her to look like the queen she was.

He agreed to let Rudy, Sharon, Kita, and Neatra work in the trap houses, on the condition that they abide by the rules. Rudy and Kita were the only ones willing to sit in the trap house in their panties and cook and bag up the coke. Two guys with machine guns stood in the living room watching just in case there was trouble.

Nasty periodically stopped to check up on shit. He would always look at Rudy longer than he should. Chastity would wait in the car for him to come out. He spoiled her with so many gifts that she didn't even have to touch the money that she had left.

Her friends, on the other hand, were running low because they were still trying to live the life to which they became so accustomed.

"I thought Chastity said that we were a team. We in here slaving, while she's riding around in Bentleys and spending money on shopping sprees and shit," Kita complained.

"You know her man ain't gonna let her work in here with niggas fantasizing over her body. We won't have to be here too much longer, once Chastity finds a supplier."

"This is bullshit though, so stop sticking up for her. She's the one that said either we all do it or none of us," Kita said.

Rudy just kept bagging up the coke, but thinking about the fact that her sister was telling the truth. Deep down inside, Rudy was feeling envious towards her best friend. Chastity gets everything she wants, while they all have to work like hell to get it. She wanted to be in Chastity's shoes, but she brushed it off thinking about how far she came. She really thought that Chastity deserves all the happiness in the world. The secret that they shared about her past, she promised to take to the grave with her. No matter what, a promise is a promise.

"I'm not taking up for her, Kita. I just think that you are jumping to conclusions about this. We're gonna be straight, you can believe that," Rudy said, trying to minimize the situation.

* * *

Chastity and Nasty were eating at Red Lobster on Baltimore Pike when Chris walked in with his wife, Nyia. They walked passed them as if they didn't even see her and sat a couple of seats down from them.

"That's crazy, how she can just jump from one hustler to the next," Nyia said, as the two locked eyes.

"It's cool, because that bitch will never make any money on these streets again," Chris replied, as they ordered their food.

Chastity wanted to ask Chris to please plug her back in, but her own pride was in the way. She knew he wasn't gonna budge, especially now seeing her there all hugged up with Nasty.

"Are you okay, ma?" Nasty asked, snatching her out of her thoughts.

"Yeah, I was just wondering why they didn't speak to me. I guess they're still a little bitter about me leaving his brother."

"Who?" Nasty asked, looking around.

"Right there. That's the dude that is planning on running you out of town," she said, not realizing that she started something.

Nasty looked at Chris, but didn't respond. He pulled out his phone and dialed a number, as if he was texting somebody. After he finished, he stared at Chris for another minute and then started eating his food.

"You don't have to worry about nobody running me anywhere unless I choose to leave myself."

"I know, baby. Let's enjoy the rest of our night, and when we get home, I'm gonna enjoy watching you run like a bitch," Chastity said, sticking out her tongue and making it turn in circles.

Nasty just smiled at the thought of her sucking on his dick. He couldn't wait until they got home, that's if they even made it that far.

"Girl, keep playing with me, and we're gonna sneak up in that bathroom. You know that you're a screamer," he said smiling.

"Whatever, nigga. We gonna see who the screamer is later."

They enjoyed the rest of their meal, before heading home to have some fun in private.

Chris wanted to approach Nasty, but he didn't want to do it in front of his wife. He was definitely going to see him when the time was right.

* * *

"Count time, to your doors," the correctional officer shouted, letting everybody know to go into their cells.

"Yo, I'll holla at you after count. Bring out everything that you want to cook with," Hakeem said to Meech.

"Alright, see you then."

After the correctional officer counted, they started passing out the mail. When the female officer approached Hakeem's cell, she gave him five letters. She was about to head to the next cell when she turned around and came back.

"Mr. Wright, you have to sign for this letter. It's from your attorney."

Hakeem signed for the letter and then opened it, first to see what he was talking about. When he read the contents, a huge smile came across his face.

"Fuck, yea! You got to be kidding me. You read this shit and tell me I'm not trippin,'" he said, passing it to his celly.

His celly read the letter from the judge, then nodded his head at Hakeem.

"You going the fuck home, dawg."

Hakeem and his celly shook hands and talked until they cleared count. When they cracked the doors, he went to Meech's cell, who was also reading a letter from his lawyer.

"Yo, you got a letter from your lawyer, too?" Meech asked excited.

Hakeem held it up, waving it in the air so that Meech could see it.

"It says that we will be getting the fuck out of prison. Can you believe that shit?" Hakeem said not really understanding the entire letter.

"Give me yours so I can see what yours says," he said, taking the letter and reading it, "It's an injunction from the courts stating that because evidence was tainted at the Medical Examiner's Office, everyone with drug cases will be released within 72 hours. You still will have to do your violation though. At the bottom it says that only cases that were affected were the ones from 2012 to 2014."

"That's me, brother, and you."

"Yeah, I'll be leaving before you, but if you need anything just let me know. We coming home dawg, sooner than we thought," Meech replied.

Meech was doing 10 to 20 years for distribution of a controlled substance. He took the wrap for his boy so that he wouldn't get 40 years. Since he had been down, he hadn't heard from his man or any of the other niggas. They did put $500 on his books when he first came in, but that was the last time he heard from them. He had been there for two years and it was about to be over. He had a vendetta that he couldn't wait to settle.

"Tomorrow morning, I'm getting on the jack (phone) and calling my lawyer to make sure this shit is official," Hakeem stated, as they began preparing their meal for the night.

* * *

A couple of days later, Chastity and Rudy were on their way home from the trap house, so they decided to stop at Nasty's house in Yeadon. She wanted to grab some money so they could head over to the Gallery.

When she pulled up, she didn't see his car outside. She drove past the house heading back southeast.

"Where is this nigga at? I told him that I would be stopping by there. Now he's nowhere to be found," Chastity said.

"Maybe he had an emergency, or he could be in a meeting somewhere. Give him the benefit of the doubt."

"You're right! It's just that it's almost time for the stores to close and it's getting dark. The nigga ain't even answering my calls."

"Let's swing passed the projects and see what Kita's nasty ass is doing. She probably has a dick in her mouth."

"They both busted out laughing. Chastity was laughing because Rudy is the freak of the squad, but she was making fun of Kita.

* * *

Nasty and his boys were sitting on the bleachers watching the basketball game. He noticed Chris talking to a couple of dudes on the other side of the court. He watched as one dude gave him a book bag, then got up and walked off.

They watched until the first game was over, then Chris and the dude that didn't leave started hollering at two light-skinned girls.

"Yo, that's one of the niggas right there that supposed to force me to leave Philly," Nasty said to his man.

"Let's go over there, and check this clown-ass nigga," his man said, ready for whatever.

They walked towards Chris as if nothing was wrong. When they were about 10 yards away, Chris turned around and stared at Nasty.

"I heard you supposed to be forcing me up outta here? Here I am now, say or do what you gotta do," Nasty said.

He stood there with three of his goons, waiting for Chris to make the wrong move.

Chris knew it was four against two, but refused to back down to these out-of-state niggas.

"I don't know what the fuck you're talking about, so you can take that shit somewhere else," Chris replied, sizing Nasty up.

Chris was a lil' nigga compared to Nasty, but he could fight his ass off. He went to the gym every day to practice his boxing techniques. If Nasty wanted to rumble, then it was gonna go down.

Chastity was about to turn in the projects, when she noticed Nasty's car parked at the courts.

"I'm looking for this nigga, and he's over there playing basketball. Let's swing over there real quick," she said, pulling in back of his Ferrari.

As they were getting out of the car, she noticed that he was about to fight Chris. She wasn't thinking too much of it, as she and Rudy nonchalantly walked towards the crowd that started to gather around the scene.

"Nigga, I don't walk away from trouble, I start it. I run these streets now. So either you can get on my team or become an enemy," Nasty said.

"Fuck you and your team, nigga," Chris said, while his man slid his hand under his shirt for his weapon.

Nasty's goons were already waiting though. They pulled out and aimed their guns at Chris and his man. The crowd began to scatter at the sight of the weapons. Chastity and Rudy stopped in their tracks, watching what was about to go down. Chastity wanted to yell out and stop her man, but the words wouldn't come out.

"Nigga, if you're gonna pull a gun out on me, then you better use it," Chris said.

He was hoping that Nasty was all talk. There were too many people around, so he figured that he was bluffing.

"What you gonna do, nigga? I ain't no pussy," Chris stated, acting as if he was about to swing.

Nasty pulled out his gun and hit Chris twice in the chest. "Boc, boc."

Before his man could pull out, Nasty's goons lit him up like a Christmas tree. "Boc, boc, boc! Pop, pop, pop, pop!"

Chastity and Rudy both took off running towards their car. People were yelling and screaming as they exited the playground. Nasty and his men jumped in their car and left.

Chris lay on the ground, breathing heavy. Blood was pouring out of his mouth, ears, and even his eyes. He was hit in his stomach and heart. By the time the cops arrived, it was already too late. Chris and his man were pronounced dead on scene.

The playground that everyone played at had now become a crime scene. Police and detectives were everywhere. They had cordoned off the entire area trying to find the suspects or a witness to identity the shooters. No one knew anything and wasn't going to talk to no pigs.

Chastity and Rudy made it to Kita's house and went inside, trying to hide.

"Oh, shit. Did you see that? That nigga hit Chris the fuck up with all those people out there," Rudy said excited. "That nigga is about his work."

"I have to call him and make sure he's okay," Chastity responded, dialing his number.

"Where you at?" Nasty said, without even saying hello.

"I'm in the projects, are you okay?"

"Yeah, I'm good. Just stay there for a while until shit cools off. I'm heading out of town. I'll call you when I get to where I'm going," he replied, before ending the call.

Chastity was home sitting in her bedroom two hours later, still shocked at what had happened. Not because of the murder, but because she had seen somebody die before… shit, she was the one who pulled the trigger. She was shocked that nobody snitched. Even though it was growing dark, there were still a good number of people out.

She had talked to Nasty a half hour ago, and gave him the update on the situation. He told her to pack a bag because he was sending her and her girls on a vacation for a week to Cancun. Neatra was the only one that didn't want to go. She was going to see her boyfriend in Chicago. They were going to leave in about a week, so Chastity and her friends were going to hit Franklin Mills Mall to shop for bikinis and other stuff.

Nasty just wanted to get the girls away from there until the heat cooled down. He was about to add a little fuel to the fire before that happened though.

* * *

A week later, Nyia had Chris' funeral. It wasn't too packed, but he did have a few friends there to see him off. His cousin had just finished singing *Near the Cross*, leaving everyone with tears in their eyes. Her voice was so soothing, that even the choir shed tears.

The pastor of the church stepped to the podium to deliver the eulogy; but before he could begin, three men walked into the church. Everyone turned to see who it was. They walked down the center aisle heading for the front where Chris lay peacefully.

They stopped in front of Nyia and her family. One man passed her a manila envelope full of cash.

"You have our condolences. That should pay for his funeral," he said to Chris' mom.

One of the other guys bent down and whispered in Nyia's ear, "Your husband was a bitch. Too bad I can't kill him again for the fun of it!"

Nyia looked up and noticed whom it was. He turned towards the casket, and he and the other two men stood over the corpse. They all hog spit on the body and then flipped the casket over, causing Chris' lifeless body to fall out of the casket and on to the floor.

Some of the niggas jumped up, but Nasty's men pulled out submachine guns. They began shooting in the air, creating a chaotic scene. The three men then turned the guns on Chris' dead corpse, spraying him with bullets. They fled through the side exit and jumped into the waiting vehicle, leaving the disaster behind.

What started out as a peaceful going-home ceremony for a loved one, quickly turned into gruesome, unforgiveable carnage.

* * *

Chastity and Rudy were rushing to pack for their trip to Cancun. Their flight left in two hours, and they hadn't even left for the airport yet.

"We have to hurry up, Rudy, Kita, and Sharon will be here any minute now," Chastity said, throwing her bikini sets in the suitcase on the bed.

"I'm ready," Rudy responded, walking downstairs.

She set her suitcase down by the door and then went into the kitchen to grab a cup of orange juice. She went back in the living room and started watching *Wendy Williams* on TV. Wendy was just about to talk about Kim and Kanye's weekend wedding when the news interrupted the show.

Chastity came down the steps and set her luggage by the door. As she fixed her skirt, Rudy hollered her name.

"Chastity, come here. There's breaking news about the prison."

Chastity walked into the living room, as Rudy turned up the volume so they could hear what happened.

"In a shocking development, a Supreme Court judge has ruled that any inmate that had drugs tested at the OCME office in Delaware, and is currently in prison due to that drug conviction, shall be set free immediately. This decision comes from in investigation conducted by the State Police where they found out that drugs had been removed from the evidence room, sparking the arrest of two employees. Anyone arrested from 2012 to 2014 is expected to be released from prison today. We're standing outside Gratersford State Correctional Institution, one of the many prisons expected to be releasing over 5,000 inmates within the next few hours. As soon as the first person steps out the gates, we'll bring you a

live interview. I'm Sarah Collins reporting live from Fox 29 News."

Chastity thought that it was just her imagination at first until Rudy spoke, "That is a lot of people coming home."

"Do you know what that means?" Chastity asked.

"No, what?" Rudy replied, not having a clue what her friend was talking about.

"It means Hakeem is coming home...."

BOOKS BY GOOD2GO AUTHORS

GOOD 2 GO FILMS PRESENTS

**THE HAND I WAS DEALT- FREE WEB SERIES
NOW AVAILABLE ON YOUTUBE!
YOUTUBE.COM/SILKWHITE212**

To order books, please fill out the order form below:

To order films please go to www.good2gofilms.com

Name:_____

Address:_____

City: _____ State: _____ Zip Code: _____

Phone:_____

Email:_____

Method of Payment: Check   VISA   MASTERCARD

Credit Card#:_____

Name as it appears on card: _____

Signature: _____

Item Name	Price	Qty	Amount
48 Hours to Die – Silk White	$14.99		
Business Is Business – Silk White	$14.99		
Business Is Business 2 – Silk White	$14.99		
Flipping Numbers – Ernest Morris	$14.99		
Flipping Numbers 2 – Ernest Morris	$14.99		
He Loves Me, He Loves You Not - Mychea	$14.99		
He Loves Me, He Loves You Not 2 - Mychea	$14.99		
He Loves Me, He Loves You Not 3 - Mychea	$14.99		
He Loves Me, He Loves You Not 4 – Mychea	$14.99		
Married To Da Streets – Silk White	$14.99		
My Besties – Asia Hill	$14.99		
My Besties 2 – Asia Hill	$14.99		
My Boyfriend's Wife - Mychea	$14.99		
Never Be The Same – Silk White	$14.99		
Stranded – Silk White	$14.99		
Slumped – Jason Brent	$14.99		
Tears of a Hustler - Silk White	$14.99		
Tears of a Hustler 2 - Silk White	$14.99		
Tears of a Hustler 3 - Silk White	$14.99		
Tears of a Hustler 4- Silk White	$14.99		
Tears of a Hustler 5 – Silk White	$14.99		
Tears of a Hustler 6 – Silk White	$14.99		
The Panty Ripper - Reality Way	$14.99		
The Panty Ripper 3 – Reality Way	$14.99		
The Teflon Queen – Silk White	$14.99		

The Teflon Queen 2 – Silk White	$14.99		
The Teflon Queen 3 – Silk White	$14.99		
The Teflon Queen 4 – Silk White	$14.99		
Time Is Money - Silk White	$14.99		
Young Goonz – Reality Way	$14.99		
Subtotal:			
Tax:			
Shipping (Free) U.S. Media Mail:			
Total:			

Make Checks Payable To:
Good2Go Publishing
7311 W Glass Lane,
Laveen, AZ 85339

CPSIA information can be obtained at www.ICGtesting.com
Printed in the USA
LVOW07s1500301115

464704LV00021B/1102/P